West of Pure Evil

Josie Malinowski

West of Pure Evil

by Josie Malinowski

OYSTER
MOON
PRESS
BERKELEY, CALIFORNIA

West of Pure Evil
by Josie Malinowski

Front cover illustration: Untitled by Josie Malinowski
Back cover drawing: *Dustball Dystopia*, by Elisa Artesero

ISBN: 978-0-578-06919-7

Additional copies of this book can be ordered from LuLu:
http://www.lulu.com

Oyster Moon Press is a non-profit, surrealist publishing co-op located in
Berkeley, California.

http://www.oystermoonpress.com

Dedicated to James Cameron

Contents

The Most Handsome Inhabitant of the Terrestrial Globe

Who wants to hear a story? I don't really want to tell you one, but I'll tell you this: the octopus is the one to watch out for. Oh yes, the octopus has ways you cannot fathom, but you should try, it's in your own interest. Eight is truly the magic number. I can hear your complaint – but the spider! What of that little minx, with her eyes and legs? Ah, I would answer you – she is preoccupied with her webs. The spider uses her legs to weave a thing of deathly beauty; the octopus, she uses hers to engender the ultimate transmutation, disgusting beauty, terrible love. There is one story I *could* tell you, which would prove it all; but it has never been told before – the secrets of the undersea should stay a mystery to we who abandoned it so long ago. But when we seek it and it welcomes us back, then may we reveal it? For our own delight and horror, how can we resist…?

Picture the old woman in her room: she's slowing down to catch sight of the only thing in the world, in the room, the once maleficent now sparse bed, its painful eyes aflame and flaccid. What's that noise? A clicking, a ticking in the wall, the clock counting her thoughts, the bomb hidden by spies, the toy frog she lost tens of years ago, an impatient ex-lover waiting for his shoes, the metronome with a life of its own, an angry candle, hissing, flickering, spitting its rage. Sit down. Sit the fuck down. She's spinning around faster than the earth, dizziness suits her, she's on the floor or the ceiling now, and the world seems right again because she's happily confused. Even if the room fills with water, it's OK, she's defying gravity and even water, once fallen, can't do it again, least not as quickly as her. The water may bring its creatures, oh yes it might, but *she* won't be afraid of them; she has knowledge of them to make a sailor shudder…

"…and so he made me salute every garment in his cabin, including all of his wife's, and told me that I had my ship back but not my crew…"

So this man was telling me, as I slowly chewed my bread and tried to look thoughtful. The story was coming to an end and I knew that any moment now I'd be expected to comment. Here he was back from Alcetia and all he had to tell me was this shit old story which a ganymede had reeled off the week before.

"…with a flask full of methane and twelve monkeys I bartered with them for a passage back, and even so I had to navigate the whole journey for them…"

I made a little sighing noise that I knew was pretty unambiguous and he paused right in the middle of his flow of speech. He raised his eyebrows. I threw the rest of the bread down on the plate and said:

"Ethan told me about that trip."

"Ethan? Ethan who?"

"You know. The cup-bearer."

"That faggot? He wasn't there."

"Don't call him that," I said. "He pays just like you."

"You've done Ethan?" he asked, scratching his head. "Well, he's obviously just doing it for show. The man's an out-and-out fag."

"Just because *you're* not man enough to enjoy your own prostate, doesn't mean no-one else should," I retorted. He didn't seem to know how to respond to that, so I said, "Are you done with the small talk? Only I'm getting a bit anxious over here."

"Sure. Unless…" he said, leaving it hanging, but I couldn't be bothered to bite, so he carried on: "Unless you want to hear the story – you know – " he leant in – "the one that sent poor Benzo off with the pixies?"

Ah, I thought, now we're talking. "Alright," I said. "I'll have a rum."

While he went to get us a drink I took a cigarette from his case and lit it with his Zippo. The men that came back from the Benzo-went-mad trip were all sworn to secrecy, on penalty of dishonourable discharge. Well – we women heard the odd rumour of course, but no man would give the full account, and no way was that from fear of reprisal. I figured whatever it was had happened on that mission, whatever sent poor old Benzo mad, was too horrifying for them to speak of; too horrifying to take into consciousness for too long, like you can't hold a man in your mouth too long, you've got to spit or swallow.

"Maybe we ought to take these up," he said, returning.

I raised an eyebrow. "A tale with sauce?"

"Christ, no. But we could be overheard."

"Whatever you want, sailor." So we went up, and do you know, I was excited enough to feel a little jolt from my lady.

Upstairs I got comfortable with a bottle in my hand and let him bide his sweet time; his reluctance to spill was apparent, but he knew there was no way back now – not if he wanted his dollar's worth, anyway – and eventually, he began.

"You know, I think, that it was a rescue mission. The captain had received an urgent SOS message from a ship that had docked at some nothing island. There were no inhabitants there, nothing worth plying for trade. The only ships that ever went to these islands were in the hands of luxury tourist companies, full of rich fucks with no imagination. They would sail out, drink on the deck till they passed out, and when they awoke they would be in "paradise". Sit on the beach and drink till they passed out again. We've had a few rescue missions from these sorts of trips. Hate taking them; the passengers treat you like cockroaches even as you're saving their worthless lives. We had only just got back from the Hawaii mission, and we were beat. In no mood to help fat old cunts. Anyway, we sailed out to the island, saw the ship a little way out. The captain – I think you know him, John Diamond – was in no hurry to get these folks back either, so he let us have an hour on the shore. Christ, I shouldn't have mentioned that detail!"

"Don't beat yourself up, Jerry. I won't remember details, and I'm not going to tell anybody anyway." My heart was racing. This was as much as anybody knew so far. If I could just keep him talking ...

He breathed deeply. "The rum is making my lips loose. I shouldn't be saying this stuff."

"You want loose lips?" I said with a laugh, and a hint of a wink. It was enough to relax him a little.

"Well, we sailed round the opposite side of the island to where the ship was stuck, and let loose a little: playing cards, swimming in the sea, simple enough stuff, but it was a luxury for us. It was such a guilty pleasure, knowing we were delaying their rescue on purpose. Knowing that we were indulging in the sorts of things those rich tourists should have been having fun doing. But anyway the captain sanctioned it – forget that, he ordered it. Anyway, after a while he called us back together and gave us the orders. We were to sail round the island to where they were stuck; then four of us, plus the captain, were to go out to the ship first of all and have a word with the crew there. I was in the bird's nest on the way over there and had my telescope focused on their ship as soon as it came into sight. It seemed strangely quiet; empty. In fact, I couldn't make out a single solitary person. I assumed they had all camped out on the beach while they waited for us. But I couldn't place anyone there either. They could have gone into the forest behind, I thought, but these tourists all loved the sun: why would they be hiding in the trees? Finally I picked up a person, a man, standing in the shallows. As soon as I saw him I knew there was something terribly wrong with this place. He was standing waist-deep in the sea, and he was naked as the day he was born. When the waves crashed onto the beach, he looked like a normal person, just standing in the water. But when the tide drew out, I could see him for what he really was. He had an *octopus* stuck fast to his crotch, its tentacles wrapped around his body. He was fucking it, slowly. It seemed to me, lovingly. At first I thought the animal was dead, but then I realised that not only was it alive, but it too seemed to be getting a kick from being fucked by this man. And it was then that I knew this place had gone wrong, so very wrong."

Jerry had his head in his hands by now. I was stricken, and didn't know how to react, how to keep him talking. Luckily for me, it seemed he had opened the floodgates and there was no way he was going to stop now.

"I didn't know what to say to the captain. I tried to remain calm, and explain in a neutral voice so as not to alarm anybody that there was something unusual about the ship. That there appeared to be no crew or passengers on the ship or on land except for one swimmer. I pointed to the man and handed the captain the telescope. He said nothing but drew me in a little closer. He said in a low voice that I was not to mention what I had witnessed to anybody, and that I was to accompany him, Phil and Benzo – who as you know was renowned back then for his hard, almost criminal attitude – to the ship. We waded out to the ship at a distance far enough away from the man so that Benzo and Phil would not be able to see what he was doing. Benzo raised a questioning eyebrow but I took the captain's lead and stayed quiet.

"When we got onto the ship we found it utterly deserted, devoid of human inhabitants, but it was all wet like it had been flooded. Each door we tried led into another empty room, dripping wet. Eventually we came to a room that wasn't empty, but by God we wished it had been, or that we could have been blinded at birth to stop us seeing what was in there. A naked woman hung from the ceiling, a thick leather strap bound around her stomach, which was attached by rope to the ceiling, and left her body suspended, face down, in the middle of the room. By her head was a huge squid, calmly watching her. By her end was another octopus, which was gently reaching up to her buttocks with one of its tentacles and penetrating her with it. I looked away, nauseous, immediately, while the captain instinctively shot the depraved beasts dead. The captain and Phil quickly took down the girl, who was practically unconscious. Me, I simply looked on, unable to avert my gaze, at the incredible scene. I could see myself being shouted at by the captain, but I couldn't hear him. He strode over and slapped me. I came round enough to hear him ordering me to investigate the rest of the ship. I don't know what Benzo was told to do.

"Upstairs I found no more signs of life. It was wet everywhere, with ink splurts here and there on the floors, walls, ceilings. I searched everywhere, but there were no more beings on the ship, human or fish, alive or dead. But on a table in the captain's room, I saw a book lying there, packed with notes, written by a human hand. It called to me. Don't ask me how, I don't know. I know I should have handed it to the captain, but by some will of

God I found myself slipping it into my jacket and taking it home with me. Whatever happened to those octopus-fucking humans, I never found out; but I did find out what happened on that ship."

I was beside myself with excitement, with disgust, with fear, and with lust. My mind wanted the story, my lady wanted the sailor, and I've always been a slave to her, so I quieted his trembling lips with the tip of my finger, and a brush of my lips. He was so afraid of the memory of that day that when I reached into his trousers he was as limp as an octopus' tentacle is in the minds of normal humans. I gave him the full beauty of the sight of my mouth enveloping his whole shaft – not so difficult when it was like this, granted – and worked my magic, my never-failing magic, but I failed.

He put himself away and reached into his bag, pulling out the book he'd stolen from the ship. Gingerly he pulled out the first handwritten note, an ancient-looking, frail old thing, which had been folded and tucked into the very front of the book. Without a word he handed it to me.

O octopus of the silken glance! You whose soul is inseparable from mine; you the most handsome inhabitant of the terrestrial globe, who govern a seraglio of four hundred suction-cups; you in whom are nobly enthroned as in their natural habitat, by common consent and indestructible bond, the sweet virtue of communication and the divine graces — why are you not with me, your quicksilver belly against my breast of aluminium, both of us seated on some rock by the shore, to meditate upon this spectacle I adore! [1]

He cleared his throat once the note was back in his possession and read the entry from the first page of the book:

"'This I found first. As you no doubt have, I took it at first to be the scribblings of a sailor too long at sea – oh, an eloquent one, undoubtedly, one whose heart would burst with the beauty and the strangeness of the world – but just scribblings, so I thought. I was so young and thought so little about myself, so little *of* myself, I suppose – I couldn't have believed myself significant enough to be especially chosen for absolutely anything. The note was handed to me, one drunken night ashore in a city whose name, damn me to hell for eternity, I have forgotten. It was in my top pocket when I awoke, and I pulled it out, read it, thought nothing whatsoever of it, and put it back. I believe I fell asleep again. Next thing I knew I was being jostled awake, it was time to work, and the note slept on in my pocket for days on end. Some time later, I read it again, and made no sense of it this time either, but I suppose it must have been stewing in my brain somehow, for I – intuitively I suppose, I can't remember assigning any worth to it at the time – folded it and put it in this very notebook you now read, which my wife had bought for me to document my time away, and I had never opened."

We sat staring at each other for a while. I knew he needed me to react the right way, only I had no idea what that was, and wasn't too confident in my ability to speak anyway. He cleared his throat again. I took a swig.

"Have you read the whole thing?" I asked, eyeing the packed book.

He nodded. "More than once. I don't understand it."

"It doesn't make sense?"

"There's so much in there…" He said it slowly, and I could see his brain trying hard to explain to me what it didn't itself understand. "This guy, the one that kept the book, was trying to piece it together. There are so many different clippings, bits of writing by different people, photographs. I don't know what happened to him, but I don't think he had it figured out by the time the book left him."

I marvelled at his choice of words. "Left him?"

He leant in closer to me. "I don't know what it is, Erin, but I have this feeling – I've got no proof though, it's just a feeling, and you know, a – what would you call it? Instinct? Hunch? I feel like this book was meant to come to me; I feel like I did when I took it and didn't hand it to the captain. Like it's – like it's up to me, like something wants me to finish this. Or maybe that I'm just the next pawn, and my fate is the same as the first man's, whatever that is."

"Are you afraid?"

"Afraid? I'm fucking terrified. I've stumbled into this, but I haven't stumbled, I've been led, I think. But I'm excited, too…My curiosity is wild, I've lost my normal passions, my rampant libido and my need to be at sea, that's why I've taken shore leave and why I-"

"Can't get an erection?"

He sat back, clearly affronted, and I cursed myself silently for my lack of tact. "Sorry," I said quickly. "I suppose I'm just confused about why you asked for me tonight if you can't…"

He hesitated, then sighed. "I guess I knew I needed to tell someone."

"Why me?"

"I trust you."

I was surprised and flattered. And suddenly, I knew exactly how he felt. It came on like being slowly immersed in warm water. Wordlessly I took the book from him, and began to read. It wasn't until much later that I realised my lady had stopped calling out. The writer had documented all his finds, various notes and articles and photos, in disparate and unlikely places, with only one thing in common – they were all about octopuses. When I was finished, I came out of the trance-like state I had been in whilst reading and found him watching me anxiously.

"This goes back a long time," I said quietly. He nodded his agreement.

"I know what we need to do."

"You do?" His hope and relief were almost tangible.

"Who would know about this? Which one person in this ridiculous place would have an interest in this intrigue?"

"Do you mean…?"

"Yes. Professor Mann."

Professor Mann was the only professor from the college in the nearby city to live amongst us savages. It wasn't the sort of place you chose to move to; most of us were trying to get away, which is why so many men turned to the navy. No-one really liked him either, which made it even more inexplicable that he chose us. People would gossip that he was an anthropologist and he was secretly studying us. They hated it, made them feel like specimens. I'd met him a few times. He came to our place every so often. Didn't have a favourite girl so it was just pot luck if you landed him. He was like the sailors, full of interesting stories, but different ones, seemingly even more unrealistic, but without the immediacy, because they were what he had read, not what he had done. Everyone knew where he lived, because everyone knew everyone's business here. To that house we made our way, and found the front door slightly ajar. Exchanging looks of curiosity, Jerry and I entered tentatively.

"Professor Mann?" I called. "Professor? It's Erin. The – uh – from the gentleman's club?" Jerry looked like he was suppressing a laugh. "Professor?" We crept further into the house. It was a state. I couldn't shake the impression that we had just missed him. We checked a few rooms, and they all had the same feeling: that someone had grabbed the most important things from them and left in a hurry. I carried on calling his name as we made our way through the downstairs, but increasingly I became sure he had gone.

We entered what was obviously his study. It was in the worst state of the rooms. Papers everywhere, books lying haphazardly across the desk, and on the floor. It wasn't what I would expect from this man, who was so careful and loving with his stories and words. It looked like it had been plundered, perhaps only moments before we arrived.

"What do you think?" Jerry asked.

I took a breath. "He's gone."

"And in a hurry. But why?"

I shook my head. "Shall we look around?"

We rifled through some of the books and papers. All of it was innocuous enough; books on anthropology, history, biology; notes he'd made on things he'd read and things he'd thought. There were a few papers written with real zeal; tiny scribbles, as if written furiously, before the ideas could slip away. Written with passion and authority.

"Why would he do this?" I asked, showing Jerry a few. Some of them were missing pages, some torn, some thrown as if without care onto the floor. "Surely he'd know what things he needed and where they were. Why would he rape the place?"

"What if it wasn't him?"

I raised my eyebrows. "What do you mean?"

"What if this thing we're chasing – what if we're not the only ones – what if he knew something, and we weren't the only ones to suspect that he would?"

"So he took off when he found out he was being watched, and they did this after he was gone?"

"Or they took him, too."

A cold fear passed over me. "Authorities, or guerrillas?"

"The former, if we're lucky."

"Meaning?"

"If they aren't like us – if they're just trying to suppress a secret, and not find it – they might have the power, but less of the intuition."

I nodded. "Science is their religion. No room for hunches."

"Do you have one?"

"There's more here than what they found."

"That's what I think."

There was a fake book. It stood out because it was unlikely, unlike the rest – pristine, unread, unloved. A fake book, and it lead me to a real space behind it. Nothing so extravagant as a room; the place wasn't large, it couldn't conceal a whole room. But there was a space there. And a space is nothing if it has nothing to fill it. But it was something. It was a space, alright. I found another book, packed with notes. I took it out gingerly, and held it, triumphant, to Jerry, but he shook his head.

"It's yours."

We didn't want to hang around there any longer than necessary, so we took the book back to Jerry's flat. Before I opened it, we got ourselves some drinks and tried to mentally prepare for what we might find.

"Where do you think he is?" I asked.

He ran his hand through his hair. "Who knows? But he can't have gone by choice. He'd have taken the book."

I pondered in silence. "What if he meant to leave it? What if he meant for someone else to find it?" We both contemplated that for a moment, and then I asked: "Shall I?"

"Take it away."

I opened the first page and read:

"Natural history has fascinated me my entire life. When I was a boy, I was already reading the ancients: Aristotle, Theophrastus, Pliny. I particularly loved Pliny. There were so many weird and wonderful tales, so many incredible explanations, but it all seemed so real to me, and more importantly, so *immediate*. I didn't feel like I was reading ancient tales, neither as a child nor as a professor, though I was berated by my colleagues for it. There was one passage in particular that always stood out to me, sang to me, such that I had it memorised, and can quote it for you now, verbatim:

"'In the fishponds at Carteia an octopus used to emerge from the sea, go to the open basins, and plunder the salted fish ... Fences were set up, but it climbed over these by means of a tree, and could not be caught except for the dogs' keenness of scent ... its size was unheard of, as was its colour; it was besmeared with brine, and had an awful smell. Who would have expected an octopus there or recognised it under these circumstances? It seemed to them that they were fighting a monster, for with its horrible breath it tormented the dogs, which it now lashed with the ends of its feelers, now struck with its stronger arms in the manner of clubs, and it could scarcely be killed with many tridents.' [2]

"'Monster', they called it, but it seemed to me it was the men who were the monsters. Why shouldn't the octopus wish to feed? Was it eating them? No! It merely wanted what nature had provided, and had found an unfathomably intelligent way to achieve that aim. I knew these creatures must be more than mere beasts or monsters. I had to find out everything I could about them, so I started collecting what was known about them by modern man and by the ancients. Here, see for yourselves-" I skipped through page after page of writing on octopus biology and behaviour, eventually coming to his narration again- "They were so intelligent – but so much more so, they were playful! Once I had learnt everything I could about them, I felt I was still missing something important. Yes, the men of science agreed they were intelligent *for invertebrates* – but emerging from the sea, climbing over a tree? Nothing else like this was documented in the 'serious' literature, in the science. And then, one day, purely by accident, I discovered something else.

"I was at a colleague's house. We were eating lunch in his dining room, and I spotted a photograph I had never before seen there. I inquired about it, and he told me an old aunt of his had recently passed away, and he'd taken the picture of her from her house, a picture of her as a young woman, to remember her by. She was wearing the most unbelievable thing: a hat decorated with the corpse of an octopus. I was dumbfounded. Why was she wearing that? He found it amusing himself, this fashion, but not as amazing as I did. He told me she had lived in Tacoma, Washington, as a young woman. I was compelled to go there.

"I spent a long time trying to discover why this woman wore an octopus on her head. I spoke to many of the older residents there, interviewing them one by one, piecing together the mystery. Transcripts of these interviews can be found later in this book. Slowly, I began to realise that octopuses do not merely use trees as pathways to food, but one particular species actually once lived in them. The arboreal octopus, as they were commonly known. They were severely endangered because their land was being decimated for logging, and because they were hunted for their decoration. Many hats, some of the ladies required, different sizes and colours for different occasions. Eventually they were hunted to extinction. I felt an intolerable sadness at this that lasted many weeks and I couldn't continue my search. But I didn't need to: the search then came to me.

"A middle-aged woman called on me one morning and told me she had heard I was interested in the arboreal octopus. She said her grandmother had loved them to fanaticism, and had written about her experiences of living in the time when they still existed. She generously gave me her grandmother's writings, that wonderful woman. It was the time of the fashion for the octopus – when they had long since been known about by the locals, and were not worshipped as the fantastical creatures that they were, but were commodities. When only the most fashionable and wealthy women wore the hats, which the grandmother was not, nor would she have owned one, she assured the reader, if she could afford it. She said that all the best restaurants had tanks of them on display, too; if a restaurant had a tank, it could charge what it wanted for rank seaweed. The grandmother had recovered from a week in jail. Witnessed the usual horrors, yet had no fear. And she said:

"'I know that the restaurant next door has ornamental tanks of octopuses all around the walls. I can't resist the urge to go in and steal one, just for the hell of it and because they are so beautiful. Stealing octopuses has become a compulsion, I've done it many times before and the restaurant is on the alert for the mysterious octopus thief, but all the same I have to do it again now despite the risk of being caught. I walk into the restaurant and am overwhelmed by the grace and beauty of octopuses wherever I look, tanks everywhere, octopuses of all sizes and colours. I take a small pink octopus from a tank and, holding it like a bird between both hands, I surreptitiously take it from the restaurant and out into the street. Its mouth parts are opening and closing gently between my fingers, it is soft and wet and I am fully conscious that I am drawn to these animals by their cunt-like qualities. I walk up and down the street with it for a little while, enjoying the excitement of the theft as well as the beauty of the animal, and then sneak back into the restaurant and return it to its tank. Back in the water it becomes white and translucent and begins to unfurl its legs. I am fascinated but I dare not stay to watch: the police will already be looking for this missing octopus, and I must be gone before they discover that it has been returned. Calmly I walk out of the front door, where a police camera man is filming all those who enter and leave the building, and I saunter back into the street, all innocence.'

"This became her passion, and her hobby. At the beginning she would steal them and return them, steal them and return them, getting caught periodically and serving jail sentences of varying length, depending on the rarity of the octopus. But later this ceased to please her. She began stealing them and returning them to the wild. Eventually she was caught emptying the richest restaurant in town of their incredible collection of the most beautiful octopuses that had been caught. She was sent to jail for a long time, and it almost ended her octopus days, and her writing. There were no entries for three years. Then suddenly, they start up again. She has been freed from jail and is finally tired of attempting to live in the society that so repulses her, so she abandons her family and goes out into the wild to live with the arboreal octopuses. She documents how she became able to communicate with them, eat with them, fuck with them. And then, her last entry, and an abrupt cessation. Is it instruction? A letter to a lover? A code? To this day, I am unclear.

"'You are wearing an octopus, like a rucksack but on the front of your body, with its arms around your neck and it bulbous head hanging down. You've been wearing it for several days, it was alive when you put it on but now it's dead and grey and dry.'

We decide to talk a walk around a nearby forest. We pass a tree whose bark on one side is quite clearly shaped like an octopus, a naturally-occurring octopus. We smile and shake our heads in amazement, unable to communicate to each other our delight.

"They didn't die out," he says. "They're still out there, and they're angry."

"Yes," I agree. "The Professor must have gone to them. Let us join their fight."

Our libidos are back now running wild, so we climb into the tree, and make intense love for the rest of the day and night.

For Lautréamont, Pliny the Elder, and Merl Fluin, who gave me words, and Paul Cowdell, Gavin Dallway, and zapatopi.net, who gave me inspiration.

Notes:
1. Le Comte de Lautréamont. *Maldoror and Poems*. Trans. P. Knight. (1978). Penguin Books.
2. Pliny the Elder. *Natural History* 9.48, 92. Trans. C. A. Ingemark. (2008). "The Octopus in the Sewers: An Ancient Legend Analogue", *Journal of Folklore Research*, 45:2.

Provided of love

As you walk past my craven window
Craving my buttered thoughts,
My mind flees to Albuquerque,
Stealing fish from ports;
My arms are bound and eyes are shut
And you watch me for yourself
But surely by now you have learnt
I'm made of spice and stealth?
Six pie-eyed flies align to dine
Upon my naked flesh.
How can you, my wide-mouthed frog,
Get underneath this mesh?
My wiry hair, my fiery cells
Conspire to stamp on you,
Preparing the last of your vices, child,
Preparing to paint you blue.

The Pig in My Soul

I looked inside, and found a pig in my soul,
where previously I thought there was just a hole.
In chains, tightly drawn round her trottery ankles,
so that the wound would fester and rankle,
she squirmed in slow breaths and fought for her life,
and asked me to spare her a thought.

'A pig in my soul', thought I, 'a pig in my soul.
Who knows what capacity this sow could hold?'
In the Biblical sense I *foie gras*-ed my pig rotten,
waiting and waiting till she was besotten.
A hundred and sixty-six years to the day,
and the bitch had consumed my libidinous play.
Bitch she a sow?? Said I bitch? Meant a cow.
And I was consuming the lot.

A sow in my windpipe, a cow in a crate,
Pomegranate ice cream, I'm pissed, that's great.
Drinking it up till she comes home to sleep
Pretending I'm comatose so I can peep
At the way that she sits on the end of the bed
Muttering about how she wants me dead.
On the brink of dreaming I hear one last thing,
And it chills my bones, as I hear her sing:
'A soul in his pig', sings she, 'a soul in his pig.
He'll be dead by the morning I'm sure.'

All Hallow's Eve

"I couldn't believe he was building the bonfire naked, his torch raised, with his family looking on. His face blushed red with heat or embarrassment, but his manner, after his father's, was one of total abandon. My child had woken up thirsty. It was one hour past midnight, but the bells were not ringing; the night sky fell upon us, dark and powerful, with the stars swarming about us, and my only daughter cried in fright at the state of the sky. He threw his fire and the bonfire exploded. We all held our breaths. Who was that laughing, and where were they hiding? An hour like a year passed and my insides burnt as the flames, and I was blinded by the figures emerging from the inferno, young girls and boys, dancing and twirling like gymnasts. On the horizon I saw a fierce gang brandishing weapons drawing near: a mass of men without end, shouting and chanting from fear borne of ignorance. I took my girl upstairs while he made music, and the fire-children danced.

I returned to the kitchen, and the blazing sky outside seemed to foretell of all the things to come that night: of the massive guerrilla warfare, of the violence and death. I, in my anger, grabbed the key to the crypt in the earth below, and brandished it at my lover just as the guerrillas arrived. Looking at me they fell silent, but soon their chant slowly started up again and grew steadily louder:

ABSOLUTELY NO PRISONERS.

ABSOLUTELY NO PRISONERS."

*For Mattias Forshage *, who wrote the original.*

* Mattias Forshage. (2007). *Frånvarande ur samma stim av bläckfiskar*. Styx: Stockholm.

Ego Frenetic; A Diotiman Mountain of Revenge

Chapter 1 – The first vote

heathens left the polling-station feeling
 that if they didn't serve fat carrion vulvas to the party of migrant venereal
diseases
a frenetic kind of war would break loose
among the carriers of this decapitating menace

Chapter 2 – The manifesto is swallowed and regurgitated

so many filthy pigeon politicians promised fumigation
 that a vicious radical pauper reverted back to the basics of human need

Chapter 3 – Things get worse

the rancid viral counts who eat themselves
 (into a malady at darkest night)
could not enervate marsupials attempting to siphon off the gases from
orgies
 fuelled by the crimes of the feudal lordships

Chapter 4 – Dwelling in the sinister mind of the vectrum

 assimilating themselves to pansexuality,
the germoids' balls exploded with excitement
so they bound their arms with rings of shedded snake skin

this caused them to develop blisters
 vile to see and putrid to smell
and so were banished to fens and swamps;

Chapter 6 – The magician

nothing was heard until a turnip-powered transistor picked up a crackling
whimper
positioned at half a mile south of the mill belonging to Jack the
Charlatan
(tight-fisted bastard of horse-jumping freaks)

Chapter 7 – Junkies march

pastiches of half-cut addicts were found quivering in bread baskets;
 they proved to be somewhat popular,
but without the fief monarchy
order could not be achieved

Chapter 8 – The coming is coming

so, fuelled by a hatred for his least favourite children
he gathered together his many blind Egos,
created his own brand of unwavering dictatorships
(called 'faith for freaks')
which was a hit with the lost halo clan of massive feet
 and tethered peacocks in the front garden

Chapter 9 – The significance

pinned to his sash was a minute buttercup,
 which loved heretics for its own depraved reasons,
and it claimed them via the impossible law stating that
zealotry can be detected by malign shades of disease
 (puce in colour)
around stomachs of bloated hags
 whose dying wish was to surround empirical laws

with their own caterpillar treaty
stating that all entrées greedily consumed by anyone with a child in a
bag
 must dictate their feverish, black, burned memoirs to a rector.
obviously this proved difficult

Chapter 9 – The number is repeated, the time to pay attention is either here or has already left in search of a more attentive audience

so seventeen cushions were sent for,
 half ordered to envelope and suffocate the dissidents,
half to blockade the fissure starting to break out at sundown;
 but they cannot pretend to venerate swans anymore,
nobody will want to protect a pea-loving switch blade
with a preference for fly-fishing

Chapter 10 – Diotima's revenge

the saw became rusty with rage,
 played a fanfare (with minute violas making up the chorus);
 a bone-tingling wail that turned compost into edible plates of horse-
meat,
garnished with a feather from a cannibal with no nipples but two extra
feet

Pieces of Sylvia

The First Piece

"I'll give you my God if you give me yours."

I stopped walking. I don't stop for preachers, but this was something else. Turning round I saw the young woman hold her hands out to me, and instinctively I took them. The pathetic look on her face told me my day was here, was her.

"What's wrong with you?" I asked her.

"I'm alone."

It didn't occur to me, this time, to look around for someone else to take the lead, to smile uncertainly at silent strangers, to walk away shaking my head in a semblance of regret.

"Come on," I said, not really knowing what possessed the words. "I'll make you something to eat."

I took her to my pokey flat, where I sat her on my sofa and got out the eggs, cheese, and ham. From the other room she sang a song, intensely sorrowful but in a language I didn't understand, and a few unexpected tears fell into my frying pan.

Sylvia was her name, but she preferred to be called Ylv: one of her many eccentricities was her preference for the middle of words. Others, I gathered over the following days, weeks, months, were that she had to braid my hair every night before bed or she could not sleep; that she loved insects with an almost religious fervour; that she believed night to be a penetrating black mist which wandered the globe once a day; that she believed some nameless god was punishing her for her misdemeanours of the past.

She lived for three months in my flat, and our routine was comfortable and unvaried; I worked and cooked, she made clothes and told me stories about people she had once known. The fantastical and implausible nature of some of these stories made me think that she was either living a hallucination, back then, or that she had stumbled into my universe from another, or, occasionally, that it was I who was hallucinating – both her and her stories.

One night as she braided my hair she told me about Guillaume, or 'Llaume' (as she pronounced it, *Yom*), a merchant-turned-monk, whom she in turn turned into a pauper – pauper in a pecuniary way, yes, but in every other way, too. She told me how she turned up at his monastery one spring evening, penniless and weary. She related to him a tale of woe (I can't say whether the tale was fictional or not) and he gave her food and shelter, though the monastery had neither in abundance. In return he asked for nothing; it was his way; it was the monks' way. He himself thrived on generosity, on giving away everything he could afford and more, at any cost to himself; in fact, the more it cost him, the happier he was. His earlier life of buying and selling, of cheating everyone and commoditising everything, had instilled in him a hatred of himself, and he now was devoted to giving, in order to purge himself of his earlier vices.

She ate everything he offered, and slept in luxury when asked if she was comfortable enough. Her deathly pallor soon turned into a healthy glow; but that soon turned into the ugly bulb of the glutton and the idler. She was not asked to help with the growing or cooking of food, and she did not offer. After three full months the other monks' patience was all spent, and they asked her to leave. She turned to *Yom*, looking for his support, and he appealed on her behalf to the abbot. *Yom* was given an ultimatum: he could leave with money and Ylv, or he could stay in the monastery without either. He struggled for days, torn between the help he so desperately wished to give her, and the help he could give the countless, but faceless, people in the future. He decided he would steal the money the monks had magnanimously raised for the woman, give it to her, and stay in the monastery. He was caught, and the money taken back. Ylv received nothing and was made to leave. *Yom*, too, was ejected, and Ylv would not take him with her, as she perceived his decision to stay in the monastery as treachery.

Ylv continued her existence much as before, sparing a meager thought for *Yom* when she saw a religious man in the street, until one day, a year or two later, when she was a little stabler, she chucked a coin at a tramp. His crusted face and repugnant clothing stirred a little pity in her, but she stopped in her tracks when she saw in his eyes the love he had felt for her back then blazing into her soul, still as strong as it was, strengthened, in fact, by time, in spite of the weakness of his body. He had smiled weakly at the woman who ruined him. She had shuddered with horror and walked away.

"I saw that I had totally crushed his heart," she said. "He had loved me blindly, unconditionally, eternally, and even in his darkest hour he smiled at me, inviting me to show him the smallest affection, and I didn't, I couldn't. As I walked away I felt the first of many pieces of my heart tear away, and fly to him. I realised I had to go back, try and do something for him; but on my return, he was gone. Where he is now I don't know, but somehow, perhaps because that piece of my heart went with him, I know he is not of this earth, anymore." I said nothing, and she continued, somewhat hesitantly: "Later that day, I saw scribbled on the side of a disused building, in a completely different part of town, the words: 'High and low, love and hate; rather both, than neither.'" She looked at me, awaiting my response.

"Even if he didn't regret it, you shouldn't feel vindicated."

"No," she agreed, but slowly. "I didn't."

As we lay in bed that night, our bodies entwined in the most sensuously and emotionally sensational way, the first stirrings of foreboding awoke in me. A fool now and ever more, I ignored them, and smelt her hair.

The City for Sale

I arrived home from work one night to find she had made me a skirt of great beauty. I had assumed she was no longer making clothes for me, as I had had nothing in three weeks; but I discovered that she had been making them and selling them, in order to buy the material for the skirt that was now presented before me. The intricacy of the embroidery was almost alien; I couldn't understand how her hands were not sore and blistered from the effort required. I put on the skirt and transformed. That evening, for the first time since our meeting, Ylv and I went out together. A humble walk in the park near my house sufficed, and we talked of idle things in perfect peace.

By the stream which ran through the gardens I ran into a friend I had not seen since meeting Ylv. He called me Val, which sounded as foreign to me as if he had called me by someone else's name; since Ylv had decided to call me Len, I had asked everyone to call me Len.

"Haven't seen much of you recently, Val," he said. He missed me recoiling at the chosen moniker, as he was preoccupied with appraising Ylv. I introduced them. Ylv smiled placidly at him, and, as I perceived it, coldly.

On our way back home, Ylv related to me the reason behind her icy greeting.

"He is the very likeness of a man I once knew," she said. "A magician and clairvoyant of great talent and immense wickedness."

I begged her tell me the story.

"I was a whore," she began, "in a city of insurmountable wealth. The sort of city where the rich can afford everything. They could purchase anything their hearts desired, anything they took the slightest fancy to. Below them the traders, who could procure whatever was desired, fancied, at the right price. And at the bottom, the human articles. Us. Me. I was living with three other whores and the magician. Benjamin, he called himself. His existence depended upon the fancy of the Rich, as did ours, and we empathised with him, though his trade was never as numbing as ours, and he enjoyed and was good at his work.

"The girl I was closest to, Elsa, fell in love with the magician, whom I called Jam. She gave him her body and expected nothing in return – neither money nor affection. He affected affection, and she took it as real, but he would waver between intense warmth and indifference; she told me it was like being in a pit that she could almost climb out of, but kept having her fingers stamped on just as she was at the top.

"A Rich also took a fancy to Jam, and decided to employ him permanently. She had him put on shows or do readings for her every night – just for her – and, I expect, more. Elsa never complained – what right did she have? He wasn't dedicated to her. But it hurt her, even though Jam claimed he only went to the Rich for a living. I even warmed to him more, for I felt he was like us now. But over time, he began spending more and more time there – staying away from our shared home for days at a time, and then weeks. Eventually he would only come back sporadically to pay rent and raise Elsa's hopes. So intense were those nights they spent together, she said, that she was convinced of his deep affection, and, though he made her no promises, she believed they would be together, some day, in the end.

"I was a little more worldly than her, and believed no such thing. I took it upon myself to find out once and for all. Knowing that the Rich did truly enjoy fortune-telling, I sold myself to her as a great necromancer, for that was the fashionable augury of the time, and it enabled me to get her alone – in a graveyard, naturally – away from Jam.

"At midnight we met, at the grave of her choice – that of her late husband. I feigned the rituals and acted as though I had made contact with his soul. I told her that her late husband did not approve of her *new one*. She asked if it was because her new husband was a Third. I said yes, and because he did not truly love her, but used her for her wealth and the comfort that that provided. She became distressed at this and asked what would become of her. I told her that he would rob her and leave her broken-hearted. As she left the graveyard, she wept, and I felt she had heeded me. I, in turn, had got what I wanted – proof that Jam had married the Rich.

"I wanted to tell Elsa all immediately, but it was night, and she was working. She arrived home just after dawn. She laughed at my appearance and I told her I was trying clairvoyancy for a change, as it had been so fruitful for Jam. Though she was tired, I told her I had to tell her something important, and bade her sit. I poured us both a good portion of whiskey – to steady my nerves as much as hers – and was about to reveal my discovery, when the door flew open and Jam stormed in. Immediately Elsa stood up and went to him.

"'What's wrong?' she asked him.

"'I've been – fired,' he replied, shrugging away her concerned hand.

"'Why? What happened?' she asked.

"I tried to slope off, but:

"'Sylvia,' he said slowly, taking in my appearance. I cursed silently. 'Why are you dressed as a necromancer?' I gave him the same excuse I'd given Elsa. A nasty, sardonic smile crept over his hateful face. 'And who was your first customer tonight?'

"'An old man,' I replied as sincerely as I could muster. The next thing I knew, my back was against the kitchen wall and his hand was tightly squeezing my neck.

"'It was you, wasn't it?' he demanded. 'You told her to get rid of me. You interfering bastard! I'll kill you!' he shouted, and he started to strangle me. Elsa, in a burst of strength I could not possibly have ascribed to her beforehand, managed to prise him off me before I had breathed my last.

"'What's he talking about, Ylv?' Elsa asked me. Her eyes shone with broken loyalty; she already believed him, sided with him, and I knew nothing I could say would change that. I spoke the truth – that I believed Jam to be deceiving her; that I went to divine the truth; that I told the Rich to chuck Jam out because I felt his actions immoral. When I'd finished Jam went for me again, and this time Elsa did not jump in to save me. Instead, she turned slowly around, picked up a hefty knife, and plunged it into her chest. As Jam tried to stem my breath, Elsa's faded out. Poor Jennifer, another of the whores, walked in from a red night to this scene. Jam came out of his rage, saw Elsa dead on the floor, and fled.

"Jennifer assumed Jam had murdered Elsa, and was trying to kill me next. I did not correct her. The authorities were notified, Jam was caught, arrested, tried, and executed. The Rich gave me some money because she felt responsible for his rage, and I was able to leave the city."

The Man Who Hated Everything

A long silence passed while the story sunk in and we wandered back home. A darkness had come over Ylv that I had not seen since the day I met her.

"It hurt you," I said. I waited impatiently for her response.

"When I came to the next town, I had something black in my heart that I desperately needed to purge," she said eventually, as we sat down to a modest dinner. "The first man I came across I shamelessly seduced. He took me to his home, and lay down upon his bed. As elegantly as a man clubbing to death his fellow soldier with the end of his rifle because his bullets are spent and the guts are hanging out of the stomach, I tore away his trousers and paused in my work, looking contemplatively at the tower I now held in my hand. His pleading eyes fixated on my thumb, which was designing its own torture, the torture of need. His will was his own, his freedom not withheld, but he was transfixed by my ministrations; he would impose nothing, decide nothing, ask for nothing. It sickened me and I put him away. His head, which had been craned to observe, fell back, thudding on the mattress. He was defeated; he retreated; he surrendered; I walked away. I did not relish in this "passion". My passion was now hatred, and I hated passion.

"Nor did it suffice when I found the men who would hit or abuse me; this was a mere semblance of hatred; after the act there would be indifference, or worse, affection; or worse, gratitude. I wanted nothing more or less than to love, and be hated in return.

"For a year I followed a fool's path, believing the more hateful I made myself, the more hated I'd be. But we humans are creatures of immense self-loathing – where I crushed a man, there would love grow. How, then, to make a person hate you? I built up trusts and betrayed them; I sold myself and robbed men; I beat them senseless and caressed them; all to no avail.

"During my search I made a living picking fruit and harvesting crops with an older farmer, whom I came to care about, and he me; we would sow crops and reap the benefits together, and it was he who showed me how to make a straw hat to shield my head from the unforgiving sun. Evenings we would spend talking and listening, and soon I felt close enough to him to tell him of my secret desire. This unique man did not judge me or even register surprise; perhaps he had already perceived in me the evil lurking beneath. To *my* astonishment, he was able to help me; there was a man, he said, who had disappeared some years ago to live as a recluse – a man who hated everything, the story went. On my behalf the farmer asked around town about the legendary man, and managed to obtain the information that he had once had a wife, who now lived in a village not far away.

"At once I begged him release me from our work so I could set out to find this man. He magnanimously agreed, and the following morning I left with a bag full of food he had pressed upon me. Three days of hitch-hiking followed, and on the fourth I arrived at my destination, a peasant village with little to offer. Asking around, I found that the wife, Roberta, lived above an inn, where she was employed as the cook. I got a room there, and stayed the night, sleep coming in fits on account of my anticipation.

"In the morning I entered the kitchens. I saw her standing before a stove, emptying bowls full of beaten eggs into a pot. On the floor by the window sat a young boy, no more than three or four, tantalizing a cat with a scrap of cooked meat. She heard the door open and looked over, then back at her work.

"'The dining room's at the front,' she said. Her accent did not comply with the villagers'.

"'I am looking for Roberta,' I replied timidly, for the woman's attractiveness and foreignness unnerved me.

"She looked up sharply. 'Yes?'

"I didn't want to approach her incorrectly – she was my only hope – so I said I hoped she would be able to grant me a small request, and that in turn I'd be delighted to buy her a meal. She turned back to the food and said:

"'I work in the evenings, eight till midnight.'

"'Perhaps at seven, then?'

"She sighed. 'Alright.'

"We agreed to meet at a rival inn, so that she could get away from hers for a while, and I spent the day in frenzied excitement.

"I arrived a full hour early, and she was already there with her son, listening with a bored look on her face to a drunkard trying to tell her she was pretty. Again I was taken aback by how out of place she looked. Out of her cook's clothing, she was even more stunning. She looked like she must have come to ruin in this place, and my hopes were elevated.

"We sat down – with her curious son – to our dinner. I told her I sought the man who hated everything.

"'Yes,' she said slowly. 'He was my husband.'

"'I must find him.'

"'Why?' she asked, and I wasn't sure whether she was asking why I sought him or why she ought to tell me where he was.

"I thought for a moment and replied: 'He has something I need.'

"Her son had said nothing; such a quiet child I had never seen, but his eyes bore into mine.

"'He left a few years ago. I'm not certain of why, or of where he went. I heard the stories about him soon after – the stories that fuelled the rumours you have apparently heard – and nothing since.'

"My shoulders sunk and I closed my eyes in desperate disappointment. I thanked her and made to leave, but she said:

"'He –' and nothing more. I stopped and waited. 'There may be a place – I couldn't say with any certainty – but if you have the time and if you are as desperate as you look, you could try it. It was a place he once talked about. A place he loved, that he wanted us to move to some day. A remote, isolated place, where he wanted us to build our own home and live off the land. I never went there. But it's the only place I know of that he may be.'

"I wanted to ask why she never went there, never tried to find him, but did not want to appear insolent. I looked at her intently, saying nothing;

she returned the compliment. Apparently she decided that I was worthy of her help. She told me she'd put me up until I looked well, and then she'd give me the location.

"For eight days and nights I slept in that inn as Roberta's guest. Such generosity I could never have repaid; she not only gave me shelter but food, kindness, warmth. And not once did she ask why I needed her husband, never did she betray the slightest jealousy or curiosity. I can honestly say I never met a better woman in my life. I repaid the favour, never venturing to find out why such a seemingly great woman could have been married to such a misanthrope.

"Eventually she decided I was ready for my quest, and she sent me off with a location, some directions, nourishment, and good tidings. In my gratitude I could do nothing but attempt to show how thankful I was by bequeathing to her the traveling hat I had procured long ago. She put it upon her son's head – he had still not uttered a word to me – and I left.

"Feverish now, I made my way south to the place of the man who hated everything. I was incapable now of human contact, and walked the entire way, existing on my will, Roberta's food, and the kindness of strangers I encountered along the way, who seemed to take me for a pilgrim. I couldn't say how long the journey lasted, whether I slept during it at all, who I met along the way.

"I found him one rainy morning, or at dusk, just where Roberta had told me – at a shore where only the seabirds dwelt, where a millennia-old tree stood taller than eight houses. A crude shelter had been built there, and before it, an impressive fire burnt bright against the rising or setting sun. The man I sought sat behind it, cooking himself some fish. He was ragged, dirty, and broken; but behind his filthy appearance I saw the trace of a man once handsome and shrewd. He did not register surprise at my sudden appearance. Instead, he looked at me, and said:

"'Will you share my meal?'

"I recoiled at once, for what man who hated everything would welcome a stranger into his carefully concealed midst?

"'Are you not the man who hates everything?' I cried, aghast.

"He sighed. 'Yes,' he said, death in his eyes but not his body. 'I hate her.'

"I finally understood, and I left with a world of disappointment enshrouding my body. He hated everything; everything was her."

I looked at Ylv over my full plate of food, transfixed. I did not really understand her story, nor knew whether or not to believe it.

"Ylv," I said softly.

"I know," she said. "I know."

I felt as though I could cry forever. She stood, circumnavigated the table, and laid her fingers on my cheek, her palm cupping my jaw. She kissed me, and my world began, and ended.

The Phantasm and The Feet Fairies

Exemplary was the word I used, when people asked me to describe Ylv. I couldn't say why; it just fitted her perfectly. I noticed that after two months Ylv was more or less my sole remaining friend in the world. But she was so much more than that too; she was my lover; my tool for living.

I began my worship of Ylv on the eve of our first kiss. I had never before even toyed with the notion that two female bodies could fit together in such perfect harmony. I had been with men; I had been with many men. I had had intercourse of all descriptions, with all manner of men. I had been to the outer edge of ecstasy with them, but nothing compared to Ylv. When her lips touched mine the world turned for everyone but me. When her lips touched mine I ceased to exist in the reality I had taken for granted; everyone I knew and loved could die when Ylv was kissing me, and I wouldn't have noticed, nor cared. Kissing Ylv was Rome; kissing Ylv was dusk; kissing Ylv burnt; she slayed me with every bite. I wanted to document each moment when her tongue was in my mouth, when her teeth grazed mine, when she grabbed my hair and pushed in closer, as though the closest we could be wasn't close enough, and she wanted to get into my skin. I realised the love I thought I had experienced in the past was a phantasm.

She did not need to make me any promises, and I asked for none. I didn't wonder how long I'd be with her. It didn't matter. With Ylv, past and future were optional concepts that had no bearing on now. She did not teach me to see; she taught me to be blind. Whether she perceived this in me is a mystery. I suspect she still had little idea of the effect she had on people; she just left behind the traces of white dust, like the creatures of the strangest tale she ever told me: that of the Eiden, the 'Feet Fairies'.

When she told me of the Eiden she entered something like a trance, and I dared not interrupt, though I suspect she would not have heard me anyway. It was as though she was narrating a dream. She was fleeing a city with a white witch, to whom she was apprentice. As they flew along on the witch's steed – a long-necked creature with white fur and wings – they skirted the grass beneath them, keeping low to the ground to keep their visibility minimal, and Ylv told the witch to be silent and listen to the grass, to the ministrations of the cricket and the earthworm; whatever dangers they faced, she said, that was the most joyful of things. No sooner had she said that than a blazing white light gleamed up ahead; a vast city, seemingly made of light. They were traveling too quickly, on too large an animal, to turn their course, and before they knew it they had sailed right into the lights. Ylv's mind blanked, and when she awoke all she could see was light.

Eight creatures, whiter than white, towered over her body.

"She awakes," one remarked. "Give her a drink." Desperately thirsty, Ylv poured into her throat the glorious liquid, more refreshing than water, more delicious than wine.

"Thank you," she said. "Where is Samien?" she asked, after her mistress.

"She could not enter," one of the creatures replied.

"Where is she?" Ylv repeated.

"Gone," said another of the creatures. "See." It held up to Ylv a crystalline eye-glass, and through it Ylv saw her tutor flying away, alone, on her steed, apparently unaware that she left behind her apprentice.

Ylv's mind blanked again and she fell into a slumber.

"I've seen you," she said abruptly when she woke again. "I know what you are. I've seen your feet."

The Eiden laughed. "She's seen our feet," they repeated gleefully. "Our feet have seen you!"

"But you're invisible. Why can I see you now?"

"See yourself," an Eiden said. Ylv looked down at her body and saw that it was light. She kicked a foot into the air, and saw that it left behind the faintest trace of a white glimmer.

"You've changed me. Why have you changed me?" she demanded.

"We have saved you," the Eiden said indignantly. "We saw you and wanted you. You will live here now; you are here, you are us."

"No," Ylv said angrily. "No." And she snatched up the eye-glass again, and watched Samien flying away at great speed; watched her progress as she passed city after city, then field after field, and mountain, and sea. Eventually Samien slowed, and landed. She dismounted from her steed and fell over in shock at the disappearance of her companion; at this point Ylv cried out the long, painful cry of a heifer dying of a neck wound.

"You took me away from her," she cried, disregarding shame or propriety or decency or care. "Why did you do it? Why?"

The Eiden looked uncertainly at each other. "We saved you," they said, but there was doubt in their voices now. "We saved you."

"Ruin!" Ylv shouted. "Ruin is what you have brought me!"

But Ylv could not leave; once admitted to the Eiden's realm, departure was not possible. She saw them; she could never see anyone again, but through the wretched eye-glass, which was her only comfort, and her torture. Every day she watched Samien; watched as she flew back over sea, mountain, field and city, asking after Ylv, calling for her, searching for her. Ylv watched as Samien grew more and more desolate, more desperate, until she had no choice but to return to the city they fled – passing the realm of the Eiden along the way, where Ylv shouted and shouted to her to no avail – and to her doom. Samien was recognised, taken away, and locked in the gaol where she was left to rot on meagre food rations and no company. Ylv tore at her hair, cursed the Eiden to the deepest circle of hell, refused to eat, could not sleep.

Ylv's cries of anguish and pain permeated through the whole city. Every Eiden felt the sorrow they had inflicted upon her as painfully as if it were their own. As Samien's strength waned and Ylv's pain grew, their ability to function as the wonderful, magical city they had once been floundered. Despair spread like disease. They couldn't release Ylv, but she was growing inside them like a tumour. More than one hundred days and nights passed in this god-forsaken manner, and finally, the leaders of the realm could stand to see their people suffer no longer: they took the only course of action left to them, and disbanded the city. The Eiden lost their invisibility, their secret lair; they became no better than rodents, foraging and scavenging, being preyed upon and dying mortal deaths. When the last Eiden had left the city, Ylv was free to go.

Her weakened body had little strength left to carry her to Samien, but she walked, stumbled, crawled, to the gaol. She let herself be arrested on arrival and bungled into the cell where her mistress lay dying of malnutrition. Samien was conscious long enough to steal a final look from Ylv's eyes, and fell away. Ylv was distraught, but comforted that Samien had at least died with a last moment's happiness. Ylv was released after a long spell in the gaol, and she lived for a year on the animals she killed in the forest ahead.

Bloodstone

Time passed, as it must, and we entered the third month of our acquaint-ance. Already I felt the stirrings of change come over her; a certain restlessness, an irritability, that I ignored or reasoned away, whichever came more easily to me.

"Can you tell me something, Ylv?" I whispered to her one night, our faces inches apart. She didn't open her eyes, but groaned a little, and the question stuck in my throat. I knew I would never again dare to try to ask it.

I rolled to lay on my other side, my back to Ylv, and as I listened to her shallow breathing, I thought.

I thought about our meeting. About how I had taken her unquestioningly into my home. About how I had listened to her story after story, never questioning, not judging. About how I had given her my audience, my food, my home, and required nothing but her company in payment. I scowled at my choice of words – payment? There should be, in no sense whatsoever, the notion of pecuniary exchange between us. But there, the thought had come to me, and I couldn't retract it.

The monk, Elsa, the man who hated everything; they had paid for their love. The monk thought that his generosity would win him love. Elsa freely gave love that did not need to be returned. The man who hated everything loved through his hate. Samien alone, it seemed, had been loved wholly, unceasingly, purely. What was it that Samien possessed? I found myself wondering, and recoiled at my own bitterness as an iota of jealousy crept slowly into my being. What had made Ylv love her where she had scorned all others? The force of Ylv's love for Samien had destroyed a city! I knew I'd never have that love from Ylv.

She stirred. "Are you awake, Len?" The sound of her voice broke my thoughts.

"Yes."

"So am I. Shall we go out?"

"Where to?"

"I know a place."

I drove as Ylv directed, away from my town, into the unknown. We didn't stop, just drove on through the night. When the first hint of dawn – that cold, unforgiving, unseeing time – approached, Ylv directed me to a left turning, and, minutes later, into the forest that surrounded the road. I had the odd, fleeting feeling that she was going to take my life.

Out of the car we got, and she took me by the hand, laughing as she half-pulled me into the thick of the trees. On and on through the forest, the dawn chorus above us deafening and wonderful, a tinge of red sunlight bathing the leaves.

"Where are we going?"

"Sh!"

I didn't speak again, and but for Ylv's occasional giggle, no sound could be heard but for the excitable birds. I was getting tired, but she dragged me on by the hand. As night finally succumbed to the full splendour of dawn, she gave one last tug, and collapsed into a clearing, where a magnificent white flower, each petal larger than my hand, grew alone.

Ylv was on the floor, laughing uncontrollably. Hysterically. Ignoring her, utterly transfixed by the flower, I dropped to my knees beside it, holding out a palm as if to touch a petal, but too awed to make contact.

"It's not possible," I breathed.

Ylv recovered herself; still a little giddy, she cried: "I remembered! I remembered where it was!"

"It can't be – it's just not possible!"

"*This* is what you find impossible? This *flower*?"

"Ylv, this is a Rafflesia – they don't grow anywhere but the densest rainforest – it's just not possible!"

"Look around you, Len!"

I looked at the trees around and almost fainted. A millisecond later, I realised sweat was clinging to my body – the humidity was astounding. The birdsong suddenly sounded different – not chirps but a million different sounds, all of them alien, and terrifying. We had fallen into a jungle.

While I was acquainting myself with this logic-defying sight, Ylv had stood up and approached the Rafflesia. With great care she circled the flower.

"Stand back, will you?"

I obeyed. She crouched down, and began carefully peeling back leaves and rocks that lay around the stem.

"It's got to be here, somewhere."

I sat down, clutching at my fast-beating heart, watching as her efforts became less careful and more frantic. Soon all leaves and rocks had been discarded, and she was clawing at the dirt beneath with her nails.

"Ylv-" I began, wanting to stop her from destroying the amazing plant.

"Be quiet. Ylv you say, but it wasn't always – If, If, that's what it used to be – when there was chance, and hope..." she was muttering. I thought her sanity was oozing out of her, as she dug her fingers into the ground, and flung piles of earth behind her.

Her face turned red with the exertion, or the apparently futility.

"It was *here*!" In a final, desperate attempt to find whatever she was looking for, she grabbed the stem of the Rafflesia with both hands and yanked the defenseless plant out of its home, the effort of the task sending her flying as it finally yielded. Coldly she threw the flower away from her, and stood over the hole in the earth.

"It was here," she repeated quietly, and collapsed.

It took every ounce of strength in me to drag Ylv back to the car (with the stem of the flower between my teeth), and every little bit of my mind to remember the way, but I managed it, and I drove us home, me exhausted, confused, and afraid, Ylv unconscious, her face bloodless.

I called a doctor, who gave Ylv a shot of adrenaline and told her to rest for a day or two. During that time we did not speak; I fed her and left her alone with her thoughts. When she was ready, she got up, bathed, and sat opposite me, in her favourite chair, in front of the electric fire.

"If, I was called," she said slowly, staring at the fire. "Because I was full of promise, of hope. Because I embodied possibility."

"Yes," I said.

"Afterwards, I called myself Ylv. Like If, but not." She smiled humourlessly. "I realised I didn't need it any more, so I left it there. I thought I could retrieve it, if I ever needed it again. But it's gone, Len. It's not there."

"What did you leave?"

She looked at me in surprise. "What do you think? My heart."

I glared blankly at her, and she smiled again, but it was a weak, imperfect smile. "You've already seen the scar."

I had seen *a* scar. A line across her chest. "I thought it was an operation."

"Well, it was."

"What exactly are you trying to tell me here, Ylv?"

"That I cut out my heart and left it under the Rafflesia."

"And so, in your chest-"

"A stone."

I blinked. "I saved the Rafflesia," I said, not knowing how else to respond.

"You did?" she said, her head perking up. "Why?"

"Because it was so beautiful."

"Where is it?"

I hesitated.

"I won't hurt it," she protested. "I just want to see it."

I pointed out of the window to my garden, where I had planted it. She stood and went over to gaze upon it.

"Just like you," she said, and this time her smile was genuine. "Anyone else would've put it in a vase."

I felt my face flush with pride.

The Blackstone Gate

But it died, of course it died, though not in the manner I could have predicted.

"It's been reclaimed," said Ylv, when I awoke one morning to find our Rafflesia disappeared overnight. She nodded her head slowly like a sage. "It was only to be expected." But not by me, evidently.

"By whom?"

"Well, it's only natural they'd want it back. Len, you are so naive, sometimes."

"Who? Who wanted it back?"

"Well, the Rafflesia guardians, I expect."

I sighed. Had it been a week since I had begun to tire of her tales? Had my weariness begun when the Rafflesia arrived? Try as I might, I couldn't pinpoint it.

"And who are they?"

"The guardians grow the Rafflesia, Len; grow it, cultivate it, protect it. Their gardens are really something to behold. Rafflesia don't just grow anywhere, they all come from that garden. The Rafflesia Garden."

"Then how, may I ask, did one come to reside here, the guardian rather than one guarded?"

"Anyone may present themselves to the Rafflesia guardians and ask for a flower; but only a few will be granted."

"And I suppose you went to them and were granted post-haste?"

She shook her head sadly. "I went to them, yes. But it was a long while before they would grant me a single flower."

I sat back, anticipating a story. Admittedly my curiosity was stoked; this could be the one time she would divulge to me the reason she cut it out in the first place. She had been reticent on that so far; and a suspicious part of me couldn't help but wonder whether this reticence was a mark of the depth of her hurt, or her mastery at weaving tales, leaving me wanting more. For how long could there be 'more'?

"The entrance to the Rafflesia Garden is flanked by two stone plinths. They are made of Blackstone, circular, and wider at the top than the bottom, so that they look like inverted top hats. Atop these two stones stand the Garden guardians – they are the guardians of the guardians. They are like little red imps, with small bodies, and large teeth, but seem less fearsome than you might imagine, hidden as they are behind gently mocking smiles. Between the two guardians stands the only gate – the rest of it is protected by a vast impenetrable wall – of black iron. They saw me coming from far away and held me with their little black eyes until I was close enough to speak.

"'May I enter?' I asked of them, and they laughed.

"'No!" One of them giggled. 'Not in your lifetime!'

"'How may I enter?' I tried.

"'This gate is held fast by the bond between us,' the one on the left said. 'Unless one of us steps down, the gate stays shut.'

"'Will you step down, then?'

"'Not likely!'

"I had not anticipated an easy entry, so I said, unperturbed, "What will make you stand down? What is your price?'

"'Price?' the one on the right spat. 'There is no price!'

"'There must be something to make one of you stand down! What is the use of a gate that cannot open?'

"'No use at all," the left one conceded.

"'Then there must be a way.'

"'How logical of you!' cried the right one gleefully.

I thought for a moment. 'My name is Ylv-' I began, but they immediately fell over laughing.

"'Idiot girl!' shouted the right.

"'Foolish girl!' shouted the left.

I was too broken to take notice of mockery and I held their gazes hard. 'My name is If,' I corrected myself, and they fell silent. 'My name is If and I need a Rafflesia to protect my heart outside of my body.'

"'Why can't you keep it in your body?' The left one seemed truly curious so I turned my attention to it. In my peripheral vision I saw the right one do the same.

"'Because in my body it is turning cold. In my body it is going to die. I need the protection of the Rafflesia to keep it safe until it is ready to return to my body.'

"'Everyone and everything dies. Why should you be different?'

"'Because I would not be dead in body or mind; I would be alive, carrying around a decaying heart. A decaying heart driven by a heartless mind.'

"'What made your heart so cold?' it asked.

"'I can't tell you that,' I said.

50

The right one, who had been silent for a while, suddenly scoffed: 'Ha! You come to us for our help and you conceal your need?'

"'No, " I corrected it. "I will explain to you my need. I will explain it in every conceivable detail, if you wish it. But I cannot explain to you the genesis of my need.'

They were silent; they awaited my explanation. I took a deep breath and began: I told them about the destruction I and my dirty, rotting heart had wrought from the moment I began to lose it until the time I stood before them pleading my case. I told them of my stories, Len: everything I've told you, and so, so much more. The Rafflesia Garden was not subject to mundane dimensions or human need so I could not say how long I spoke; but I told them all and omitted nothing and they listened to every drop.

"When I was finally spent the left imp looked sadly to its companion, who was stubbornly looking away into the distance. 'It is greater,' it said quietly. The right one said nothing. 'Is it not?'

"After a few moments' silence, I timidly asked: 'What is greater?' And the right imp looked at me, and the desolation in his eyes was terrible to behold.

"'We only step down when the need of the one who would enter is greater than the love one of us feels for the other.'

"Horror welled up in me and I broke down onto the floor, wailing and cursing myself for causing destruction even here when I sought the means to end it. The left imp stepped slowly off its pedestal and the gate disappeared at once. I couldn't bear to see what would become of the two imps and so I stepped straight away into the garden."

As Ylv finished her story she was looking wistfully out at the empty spot where the Rafflesia had been. The next day I awoke to find her gone. She had left nothing, as she had brought nothing.

Dedicated to the exquisite pain that is love.

Carpet-cleaning ho-bag

It was like shitting on a stick. No point to it at all. I was having a decent enough day; as decent as they come in times like these. I wasn't getting as much sex as I'd like, but who was? Around that time I was toying with the idea of prostitution, but I didn't think it'd sate me, what with the demands of the job and all. So I stuck to sales, door to door, which was alright. I could talk as much as I wanted, and sometimes got a cup of tea or a fuck. This time, the door had opened to a man in his thirties, so I thought, unemployed, kids off to school, wife off to earn the dough, he in his pants watching porn. I took it as a good omen that he didn't turn the sound off when he opened the door, and I started working my routine. But looking down at his pants, all I saw was flaccid, and I didn't really have the energy to try to seduce him. He was a lost cause. No point. Like shitting on a stick.

But where there isn't a shag there might be a sale, so I tried the pitch instead. I guessed his stubble was three days old. He looked like he might have washed more recently. No great candidate for carpet shampoo.

"It's pouring. Come in for a cup of tea," he said. No sex, no sale, but tea. Not a total loss. "Do you want sugar? Or would you prefer coffee? Or something else?"

I smiled placidly. "What else can you offer me?"

He shrugged. "We've got a bit of everything. I'm on beer, but I guess you can't drink."

"Never assume."

Smiling, he handed me a cold can. We sat in his living room. He muted the porn, but didn't open the curtains. I wasn't there to judge him. Who the hell was I, anyway?

"What did you say you're selling?"

"I doubt it matters."

"There's that power of assumption," he said with a smile. "Fucking hypocrite."

"Hm," I said, and took a swig. "Carpet cleaner."

"We've got some. I'd ask you to repeat your pitch, you know, to humour you. Only if you want the practice, though. I'm quite busy, as you can see." He gestured to the TV.

"Sure," I said. "Superficially."

"Meaning?" I glanced meaningfully at his crotch. He followed my eye and caught my drift. Laughing, he said: "Your implication bothers me. Can't an impotent man watch porn?"

"Can a blind man see the stars?"

"I see them alright."

The ensuing silence was awkward. I looked unhopefully at his acceptably clean carpets. My carpet cleaner voice kept saying to me that I wasn't going to go superthreshold this month. Commission threshold. I was so fed up of that voice I wanted to dive into oblivion.

"Shall we do small talk or shall I drink my beer and fuck off?"

"I'm not on a payroll, I don't care too much either way."

"Married?"

"In the Biblical sense."

"Children."

"The same."

"Content?"

"In no sense."

"Hopes?"

"To find some."

I was all out. Energy was seeping out of my fingertips like the rain outside, and I was especially tired of similes. I shrugged.

"Your turn."

"Husband no; children no; contentedness sporadic; hopes…daily."

"What fascinating creatures we are."

"I am a creative of my own device. I blame no one."

He raised his eyebrows. "You want to have sex, don't you?"

"Generally."

"Shame. You thought about porn."

"Sure."
"Me too. Shame, though."

Oberone

Oberone, Oberone, my death barberette
You may yet quantify these suffragettes
Your tongue may be icequeen and deliciously wet
But I'll have you my love, I'll have you yet.

Peregrine, Peregrine, my old antique face
Pass me that canister filled full of mace
I've eaten the cherries and I'm tied up in lace
And locusts are swarming, devouring this place.

Silverine, Silverine, you unctious headfuck
I've just been bitten by old lady luck
She's licking my feet and starting to suck
Oh please come and join me, you nubile young buck.

Yolutude, Yolutude, where have you been?
Miserly topedoes are bashing my spleen
You must give me more pilchards, ones that aren't green
For underground fruitbats are usurping the queen.

Being spice

"Assuredly I'm six," said the man to his wife;
"I'll slap your six dicks," she replied.
"Come round here once more with your jam-sodden feet
 And I'll heat you with meat till you're ready to eat.
 Then I'll flay your brown hide,
 And forgetting my pride,
 I'll fuck your remains till I've died."

"Quite certainly you're mad," said the boy to his dad;
"I'll choke you, wee lad," he replied.
"I'll just finish this puzzle then I'll break out the ice,
 Then I'll slice your fine eyes till you've stopped being spice
 And I'll paint your hair white,
 And when you're all right,
 I'll fly you at night like a kite."

Martyrdom

"Fly away, you fucking idiot, fly away!"

This is not the time to be mincing words, I thought.

"Whither shall I fly?"

"Yes, whither! Now fly!"

Katherine stood up and flicked her cigarette at me. "You're a moron. See you tomorrow."

I watched her slope off, the dark particles of night enshrouding her figure until I was blind to it, and then it was nothing but a memory and a wish. I slumped, my back resting painfully against corrugated iron, picked up her depleting fag butt, and sucked on it greedily, savouring the nicotine, relishing in my thirst, tasting the lip balm she left behind.

"Come back," I croaked, knowing I said the words only to alleviate the silence. "Martyrdom," I whispered, disdainful. "It's overrated, you know. And more drawn out than you might think."

A rat sniffed the toe of my boot, then nibbled it. I flicked my fag butt at it. "Fly!"

Rules of the inn, 1786 (found poem)

No thieves, fakirs, rogues, or tinkers.
No skulking loafers or flea-bitten tramps.
No slap an' tickle o' the wenches.
No banging o' the tankards on the tables.
No dogs allowed in the kitchens.
No cockfighting.
Flintlocks, cudgels, daggers, and swords to be handed to the innkeeper
for safekeeping.
Bed for the night 1 Shilling.
Stabling for horse 4 pence.

Found in The Lugger, a pub in Fowey, Cornwall

Caterpillar (Close Your Eyes)

Close your eyes. What can you see?

Fire. Fire dragon mothball soup.

Ok. What else?

Green doctor rocks defile patients prosthetic satchel of plasters.

Maggot leg-man axe fasting open table greying soon kill beacon tremble wood.

Blast smoke sky scream hat grass brown hold bed cliff uniform burn cry gun green.

Now?

A hundred tiny parachutes carrying tiny bombs. A battlefield. Women. Men. Slow descent of parachutes. Someone's running down the hill. His hand. His hand. His hand. Oh, fuck. A burn hole through his hand. Sizzling and smoking. He's screaming. There's no hope for us.

Good. So he's been hit by one of the parachutes?

They've stolen our shoes.

Who?

The daughters of vicissitude and money, flapping wings among giant eyes out of rock surfaces, it's he, the troll, or the trumpet-blower to the admiral

Who?

Fiery red guerrilla armed forces destroying climbing into my skin crawling through to third generation stomach arm nails scratching up to chest panic and terror it was him he did it!

Who did it?

Oh God he's got her liver I think I'm going to vomit he's thrown it over the wall oh God it's squelchy, bladder-tennis, I

Yes?

Caterpillar. I've got it. It's in my palm. I have him. What do I do?

Where are you?

Wait, don't! It's a trick!

Shit, shit, shit shit shit, she sacrificed herself, it locked its jaws onto her neck, there was no hope, heard the crack neck breaking

Fisticuffs!

We're past the giant centipede. My hat fell off. We're going up the stairs. I'm at the door.

Is the caterpillar ok?

He's fine.

Go in.

We're in. Lights, lights, lights everywhere but nevertheless a polar bear dancing oil lamp shaped necromancer pirouette he's one of us no problems he's going to take us to the room what's that light...

Go with him.

No.

Go with him.

I'm refuelling my Zippo.

Where are you?

Bedroom. Wiping oil off hands with tissue oil is tissue I am not flammable looking out of window a girl, one leg in trunk lifts head sees me but no fear no disquiet just face, they're behind me titter titter point and sneeze, I've noticed you, I just want to reach for my cigarette...

Who's tittering?

..and I've got it and it's in my lungs now she's opened the door and in and drive away, I can imagine it

What can you see now?

A man in a tree with no name.

What is its name?

Is doesn't have a name.

What doesn't have a name?

Its name is Jack.

Whose name is Jack?

The polar bear is brown. He waltzes down a long straight corridor and

I follow, with the caterpillar in one hand, the umbrella in the other, the sheep, the bare-bottomed horse, the ant-eater, the fire-cleaver, the moose-milkman…

Where are you going?

We're tangoing down the corridor. As I turn the corner, a muffin.

The polar bear has stopped, he's pointing at my hand, he's noticed the caterpillar, he's screaming, he's not one of us! He's calling for guerrillas! They'll be here soon, we must go quickly…

Hurry now.

A prostrated blind rubber band at my feet. Why?

I don't know.

The caterpillar ate its toe.

He's vomited. It's black. He's laughing.

…

The guerrillas turned the corner, they're upon us. What should I do? What should I do? What should I

Go into to room quickly and shut the door.

In the room!

A room of neon circles tubular newts in pickle jars, she's in the middle of the room

"hot hot hot but don't forgot

I damn them all to my chamber pot"

She spins around, a tutu.

I place the caterpillar on her head.

What happens?

The guerrillas have knocked the door down! They're swarming the room! They drag me by the collar, one blindfolds me, I hear shouts and screams, they shove me forwards and I collide with a wall, they turn me around to face them I cannot see, black black blackness, I hear a click they're loading the guns! Firing range! Death by! They're about to fire! I'm going to die!

Don't panic.

But I'm going to die!

I'm here.

They're shooting!

What happens next?

What happens next?

The caterpillar's hair had re-grown so I took him to the depository for a brief check-up, just to make sure that everything was, as I was assuming, going in accordance with current British law, but when we got there was a rather large centipede in place of the guerrilla guardsmen; no less fearsome and far more arbitrary.

He didn't allow us to cross the border, we didn't have enough pens, he said, our minds were not suitably filled with television theories, and besides which, we did not know the password – well of course not, his password was different to the guerrillas', and nobody had told us what it was.

Days, seconds, later I was squaring up to the very same man and he was part of the concubinage of the 70s – quite unexpected as you can imagine, a huge phallus, never expected such an erect building as this! he cried, and the tears flowed until dawn by which time I had challenged him to fisticuffs and beaten him hands down.

Foraging through the standard nuts and berries, my hat fell off and he raised up to his hind legs, showed me his slimy underbelly and cried, "I myself know how you people work, you'll never fool I, I the great one, shall endeavour to vouch for your reprisals!" With that he slugged off, to my disgust, with a lady caterpillar, the very same one I had arrested at Easter for stealing my van.

It was a rather fortunate event, and I decided it was time for tea, with cucumbers, being that I hadn't fornicated for so long and I did so miss those times, so we congregated under a bilberry bush until it was safe to enter.

Lights, lights, lights you may hear, but nevertheless a polar bear, a nifty oil lamp shaped necromancer, he can dance, I cannot sing, and together we made the quartet commonly known by its chemical name, a fire-eater, a sheep, a bare-bottomed horse, and all together we made our way to the desert.

No and no, and all the same why?

Plethora of sperm, what's going on in this land of crap, asked the polar bear. Caterpillar took the fort and replied, 'I ate my toe because they told me to and after all it was I who once ruled over that man, he did all I said, he made me so that I could be able to misinterpret a whole variety of frogspawn, the little red fiery dragonballs, they placated us for a while and stole our shoes, a crafty plan to be sure, but we had our tea under a small umbrella by shrinking into tiny little men of servitude – not the kind you find on the back of cereal packets, no indeed, it was as inbred as a cacophony of Dolly Partons, if you can imagine such a thing; I certainly can't, but I was having a day of mourning, you understand'.

I swallowed the arm dangling from the ceiling, fingers down to stomach, nails scratching my innards, I'm quite full now thank you.

Let me get back to the caterpillar; he was sick, sick as a shoe, sicker than your mother and a fideldeedee (but who's counting?). He vomited black tar on the floor right in front of the guerrilla and the gorilla laughed, he shrieked and pointed with his pickle jar, but of course he had no idea who the caterpillar was, he couldn't have foreseen the repercussions of his ill-timed bet, and the caterpillar laughed right back at him, and I'm standing there thinking, what shall I have for dinner tonight? but before I can even approach the question a marsupial swans out of the steps on his periscope, what a sight it was, even the blind rubber band prostrated himself, such was the awe flying around the place.

We swam in through the door and a fairy. She spun on her tippy-toe faced meat cleaver, singing a song of merry Mary Magdalene, "hot hot hot but don't forgot, I damn them all to my chamber pot". Remembering my position in the otherwise crowded ensemble, I drew my sword and challenged them all 'what ho I say young boy, I purr every time I come upon your face'. 'It can't be you!' So the guerrillas, pushing and mooching with any member of the royals, by whom I mean the prince and his sauce the prime monster, gathered one and all for the execution of the lot of them, a bang and a whoosh and 'hey diddlydeedee, an actor's life for me, stuck my cock in his wife, a blow job and it's over', and yes by Jove, it was.

"Did they…?" she trailed off. He nodded. She could smell his sweat. His shaky hands lifted a cigarette to his mouth. "Shit!" she shouted, banging her fist on the table. She looked at him. "Tell me everything," she ordered.

"I can't. Give me a second. It was a fucking massacre. I need a drink. Can I get a whisky?"

"Afterwards. Tell me. Now."

He shook his head and began to cry silently. As his shoulders shook, she stood up, drew her arm back, and slapped him across the cheek. He looked up at her, tears and sweat and saliva shining on his pale skin.

"OK," he choked. "But I want conditions," he added defiantly. She started to raise her hand again, but caught herself, sat down, and took a deep breath.

"What conditions?" she asked slowly.

"You can't hold me accountable. I have no more to do with it. You let me go home," he said, looking down at the table.

"Agreed. Now what happened?"

He began to wail. "Dead, they're all dead," he sobbed. She stood up, took a long metal stick out of her draw, and poked him with it. He screamed, fell on the floor, convulsed. She sat back down and folded her hands on the table. He shuddered as he stood up, ran his hand through his long hair, and sat down. He cleared his throat.

"We're not sure how they got him," he said shakily, "nor how they gained entry. We were alerted by cries from Lieutenant Colonel Toulouse. We ran as fast as we could...but – but – but..." he put his head in his hands and sobbed. "Just let me go home!" he screamed. "I did what I had to do! Why don't you let me go!" he stood and ran to the door, tried to yank it open, but it did not move. He turned and looked at her with murderous eyes. "You said it wouldn't be locked."

She shrugged. "Do you want to go home, or not? Tell me the rest and I assure you I'll let you go."

He dropped his head in defeat. He walked back to the chair, and sat down. He put his elbows on the table, his chin resting on his hand, and he looked her in the eye.

"We killed them all. Blindfolded them. Lined them up. Loaded the guns. And fired."

"Then why is every one of my fucking men dead except you? Why? Why? Saved your own neck did you? You fucking coward! You disgust me!"

She pushed a button on the desk and a buzzing noise sounded. The door burst open and two armed guards stood either side of the doorway. The man turned around, and, seeing them, grabbed her hand and began to plead:

"You said I could go home! I haven't finished the story! Wait" – he swallowed – "let me just finish telling you what happened. You'll see it couldn't be helped. Just five minutes I'll tell you what happened and then I'll go home!" he forced a smile. She nodded, and the guards left the room. The lock clicked shut.

"They - they got into the room before we reached them. The minute we got there we seized the lot of them. But he's so small, isn't he? I mean, we just didn't notice, none of us did...anyway, we lined them up, as I said, and fired, got them all. But we didn't realise she was behind us. Even if we'd have seen her, we'd never have thought....but they'd already got her. I was the first to notice her. Thought she looked a bit weird, scared, even. Never seen her like that before – well, we wouldn't have would we? So I started to nudge Doug – I mean, Private Wood – but as he was turning round, she let rip. I ducked. No one else did. They all went down. As I was crouched down, I fired. She went down. I stood up, and everyone was dead." His face screwed up as he began to cry again.

She stood up, grabbed him by the collar, and pulled him towards her, until their noses were barely an inch apart. "She's dead?" she muttered through clenched teeth. He nodded. "You killed her?" He nodded again. She threw him back down onto the chair.

"You stupid cunt," she said slowly. He sobbed quietly. She pushed the buzzer. The armed guards burst back through the door.

"What?" he screamed, looking at them. "But you said I could go! You said I could go home! You agreed!"

She looked at the guards, nodded her head, and turned away.

Molière is having a soirée!

Molière is having a soirée!
He invited me, I'm Rio Marè
He's holding it in the underground church
Where the wartime fruitbats lurch.
He served up shots of tequila-milk
Which crackle in the throat and taste like filth
And at about a quarter to three
He made an honorary pass at me.
"Being a sailor is a profession, not a career," (he said)
As he stroked the cum on his mushroom head
And I felt a tingle in my sexual cells
And I showed him how to ring my blueberry bells.
We each had a bolus of mianserin
And he said, "It's all about connecting things,"
As he carefully joined together two spider webs
With his gentle, sticky fingers.

Lollipop shop

Forcible stationary is white when you prefer to pick up the facelit from the housing estate, three miles around the diocese there were pinnacles of spit crying out, like banshees. A rancid yellow snowdrop fell blindly with no regard for the twelve young centipede maidens eating orange bows. When I called to pig, he replied 'but only if your dangling heart will elevate my eyes'. I couldn't comply, my face was burning rice, and no-one would rescue wigs from the lollipop shop. Rainbows bounded over the hospital roof, claiming the land as their own, frying giant tortoises just because they wouldn't mention pacman's name in the witness box. It was unfair and we all cried into our bottles of acid, diluting them somewhat, and they were less effective in spinning apples across the universe. Gestational tigers ran away from the fray, maiming vipers who were only there to observe the police. Oblong were the weapons, both u-shaped and l-shaped, but not, not ever, loaded with hazelnuts, only pellets made of bird spit. Thrashing the captives with the horse's tail, the chief bartender wondered how his life had become quite so sadistic and he found he enjoyed the ride on the spiral man that had been bequeathed to him a year ago. People shouted for their queen, shouting 'queen, I smite you', wearing badges.

All the kinds of love there ever were

The single malt is in my hand
It's sticky and it's wet
Oh how I love it when
You strangle the vet
Oh how I love your nose
Your stupid face and dirty clothes
Oh how I love your cock
Shooting in another sock
That goes back in the drawer for me
And makes my shoes smell nice.

Witching Hour

It wasn't long before tiny mouths began to sprout all over my bodily skin and I was cackling all over, heathen though I may be I still had a sense of humour, even at this witching hour, when they came and emptied their cauldrons over hot ash-cakes made with sour raisins. I wasn't actually terribly hungry so I decided not to hang around, though with curiosity piercing my breasts similar to the longing I felt for my lover, I revolted against my desire and stayed after all. First they appeared not at midnight like I was led to believe but after 3am, when I was becoming weary and I was all out of mushrooms with which I had intended to placate them, lest they hear my incessant mirth. Second they flew not upwards but across, their feet barely leaving the floor and only levitating the height of a matchstick. By the time they pulled out their breasts to bare to their master, who turned out to be me - who knew? - I was highly disappointed and was sorry I'd forgone a night of debauchery only to be made god to a bunch of wannabe-martyrs.

The sky was lit purple with their wretched song and I overcame many obstacles to get away from those tenacious bastards. They'd set up a trap for their own deity, intending to force me to bestow on them my eyelashes and frogspawn from my garden.

'Bestow, bestow,' my little mouths mimicked, and they grew angry. As if they didn't know those little mouths represented their own ridiculous wants! I began to grow nauseous and warned them that I may soon vomit on their precious gowns.

'Do it!' one of the men said, clearly erect, and my little mouths mimicked,

'Do it! Do it! Do it!'

I was running out of patience fast and needed a quick getaway, so I gobbled them all up and washed them down with the ash-cakes. They weren't half bad, in the end.

A Day in the Life of Murkrad

Murkrad: the name of a ship. *Huge* sails, and not just relative. Not relative to my ignorance. No; they were truly huge. Think of... think of a monastery. In it, there are fifteen nuns and one priest. He's a horny old toad, and even as a boy he wanted nuns in 'that' way, though he didn't realise it then. He didn't know that his night-time visions of smacking Sister Mary Joseph with her own cane were the stirrings of sadistic desire. What's a priest to do? Wear the robes, finger the rosaries with your left hand, sure. But is it enough? Can fantasy ever really satisfy?

It was only to dock for a day. Days, as cellmates will surely tell you, can feel like years. So maybe it docked for a day, and maybe it docked for a year. No-one was keeping count. In fact, in the town that Murkrad docked, people often confused days with years. They could never remember which was which – was a day the earth going round the sun, was a year a spin on the old axis? That's why it was not too uncommon to hear calls of 'See you next year!' at pub closing-time, or 'Happy New Day!'. The crew of Murkrad were not, ironically enough, ship-shape. Of the twenty-two on board, thirteen were ridden with scurvy. A fourteenth ill man had a bad case of typhus fever and was being quarantined, and two more were bed-ridden by advanced cases of cupid's disease, a present from a whore they shared some years back. Six healthy men, therefore, climbed down from the ship, with their empty barrels and their loot. Of this six, one of them was the captain. He was called Frank.

In the monastery, dinner was being served by Sister Agnes. Now Sister Agnes had been a felon in a former life, and she had a fondness for thistles. She loved to make the girls a nice thistle stew, and thistle cake as an extra-special treat. (I'd mention the thistle necklace she wore around her neck, and the thistle pants she knitted when no-one was looking and wore to bed every night, but I don't want you to judge her. Was it self-flagellation? Was it mild kinkiness? Who could say, but God Himself?) The ladies of the monastery put down their hoes and needles, and gathered one and all at the table. The priest, of course, sat at the head of the table. He was looking at his delightful nuns, thistle stew waiting patiently before him, trying to decide on whom he would bestow the honour of pre-dinner prayer. As he opened his mouth to speak, however, "Fuck!" came a cry from the other end of the table. Sister Briony, it seemed, had broken her silence. Mortified at herself, she burst into tears and fled. And now the moment you've all been waiting for. She ran out of the monastery, tears pouring out of her eyes, blinding her, and who should she bump into? Was it Frank? No.

Back on Murkrad, the man with typhus fever was playing solitaire. It was the only thing that contented him, any more. With the captain gone, he could play it on the deck, in the sun, instead of being confined to his cabin. What joy he felt a pauper in a linen suit could not say. As he was just on the cusp of winning, a mite of a shadow, unseen by our hero, crossed the wooden floor and came to rest by his feet. It whispered in the most devilish voice it could muster,

"You will give me your corpse, won't you?"

Predictably, our hero screamed. "Who's there?"

"Who's asking?"

"A servant of the King!"

"Oh no, not another one. Never mind, then." And it skulked off again. To say the man was petrified would be true. Out came his sword, but who can fight an invisible foe? Or worse, one that's already scarpered? After that incident, the man scurried back to his dismal cabin, and once he was sufficiently convinced that he'd gone mad, continued his game in the dark.

But the mite of a shadow wasn't finished just yet. It knew there was someone on board it could use. Someone with a dirty soul and no sense of justice. It could feel the presence. It knew somewhere on that ship there was a being that did not love its king, its country, its duty, and the mite wanted it.

The stowaway's palpitating heart was just starting to come to resting point. The voices of the healthy sailors had long since departed, and the barrel in which that heart resided was still on the boat. This, the stowaway was slowly starting to realise, was a very good thing. The stowaway slowly started to piece together the bits of information it knew to be true. The sailors came to get empty barrels. The sailors left with empty barrels. The sailors were going ashore. The stowaway had an issue with conjunctions; she just didn't really get them. So combining these bits of information into a coherent whole was no easy task for her. After much deliberation, she decided that, given the information she knew to be true, she must be ashore. It was a pretty nasty shock then, when she emerged from her barrel, to find she was still on the ship. So shocked was she that it took her a full two minutes to process the question she'd just been asked.

"Why? Am I dead?"

"I don't think so... You're not, are you?"

"I don't think so. What do you want my corpse for, then? I mean, I haven't got one."

"When you *are* dead, I mean. When you will be. When you're going to be dead. When you're *dead*!"

Another problem the stowaway had was with the future tense. She just didn't really get it.

"Are you saying I'm dead?"

"No! I'm just asking, if you were to die, could I have your corpse?"

And don't get the poor girl started on the subjunctive. She climbed out of the barrel.

"No-one else has asked, so I suppose you got in there first. Here you go."

The mite blinked at her. "Er... thanks. See you later, then." And it skulked off again, unsure of whether or not its trip had been successful. Miranda, for so the girl was called, waited for five minutes, and when nothing further happened, she climbed to the deck and onto the shore.

A tailor – which, you'll see, is nothing at all like a sailor, despite appearances – was in bed with his wife. He was the fourth son of a fourth son and as gay as a trampoline, but conventions had to be followed. His flaccid cock – his wife's greatest enemy – lay traitorously limp in her hand.

"It's the blood flow," she said knowingly. "It's all in your brain. You're thinking," she accused. She wasn't as stupid as she seemed. She didn't know about his predilections, and so came up with many excellent reasons for her husband's unresponsiveness that had nothing to do with him not worshipping the arse she sat on. Giving up again, she lay back and thought of the ocean.

Dedicated to the bottle of dark rum.

The last plate of food

I vowed to throw out that last plate of food
On Thursday it was top of my 'to do' list
But my 'to do' list turned into a gnome
And the gnome was cruel and arbitrary
And he carried with him a carrot
He said it was his toy
I know what kind of toy it was alright
I saw him masturbating it in the kitchen

On Saturday the carrot had triplets
And that last plate of food was beginning to grow mould
I hid under the floorboard
(Which was curiously also the hiding place for the stars during the day)
I heard the triplets squeal and bawl
And the millennia of peace enjoyed by the stars
Ended on that day.
So the stars and I
Formulated our revenge.

The last plate of food grew into a fine young man
And took a fancy to the elder of the triplets
Whom the gnome had called Analgesia
They held their wedding-ceremony in the kitchen
Where they had fallen in love
But by the evening Analgesia had grown old and weary
And rejected the last plate of food's sexual advances.

By the end of the week the stars and I were ready
We surprised the gnome at midday while he ate luncheon
The stars crept up and pulled down his trousers

The last plate of food

And I was starting to hold my belly and chuckle
When one of the stars fainted
And soon they were all out cold
And when I looked back at the gnome
He had melted into a pool of soup.

Umbrella Tyranny

She was close to the bounty-hunters, so close that she could smell the sweat pouring out of their knuckles. Kneeling behind a tree, she heard a *crunch* as her brittle bone broke at the contact, and her hand flew to her mouth to stem the expression of pain trying to escape. She knew she needed some kind of god-given miracle to save her from this predicament, and, though she wasn't the praying type, she couldn't move from her kneeling position and felt that just maybe this was the one moment in her life when it was OK to pray, given that she *was* prey. As she knelt, shooting pains coursing through her leg where the bone had split, she looked up to the heavens or the stars and asked for a miracle. What she got in answer was a speck of rain right in the eye.

"Fine, spit on me then, in my time of need – spit in my eye, bastard god!"

In answer to *that* she got another speck of rain down her back, and then one on her nose, and then more and more huge, cold drops of rain began to hammer down onto her face and body, and then, in the distance, the low grumble of thunder sounded. She looked at her surroundings. She might avoid a total soaking by the shelter of the trees; then again, she might be under a tree that would be struck by lightning and kill her. It didn't really matter anyway. She was going to be killed this night, whether by god or by man.

"I heard something over there."

The voice shouted to its companions, and she saw the three armed men run past her in the totally wrong direction. Of course they heard something over there, she thought, the thunder, the rain, the annoyed caw of the birds, and a thousand other things besides. Damn idiot fools. They were shooting arrows randomly into the canopy, and by pure luck one of them got her good leg. She stifled her cry and tried shifting her weight when the coast was clear; she found she could lift her broken leg a little now, and drag the arrow-penetrated one alongside, and position herself so that all the weight was off of them both. She huddled right into the tree, which happened to be a very big one, and managed to squeeze herself right down into a gap between two enormous jutting roots. Then with a quick glance to see who was looking she swept wet leaves on top of her, until she looked like the tree itself. Then she waited. The rain pounded, the thunder grumbled, the lightning flashed, and she waited. Animals jumped from tree to tree, birds took to flight, insects crawled over her skin, and she waited. At some point she passed out from the pain and the cold.

"Don't use water, fool, can't you see she's already soaked?"
She heard a noise buzzing in her head that sounded suspiciously human.

"How do we wake her, then?"
As soon as she thought about it, the pain in her legs came back tenfold and she winced.

"Never mind; look, she's coming round."
She allowed a single eye to flick open and saw three blobs looming over her. Death, she thought, probably, and perhaps a minion of satan, and so who's the third?

"Wakey wakey, love."
Ah, of course, she thought. The executioner, because I'm not dead yet, am I?

"That's right – open your eyes."
The light that streamed in through her pupils was so intensely bright that she couldn't tell where she was. It could have been the rays of the sun following the storm, or it could have been the entrance to hell, or maybe it was a torch light and it was still night and she was still in her tree.

"Here – she's been shot in her leg, look."
The other two shapes made hissing noises at the state of her leg. She knew it must look bad, because she could feel the sticky, congealed blood there. Maybe the bone was even sticking out. Maybe it was gangrenous, who knew?

"That must be painful."

She tried to nod and sit up, but a hand pushed her back down.

"Oh no you don't. This is not the time to speak or to move. I'm going to end your pain now, love. It'll hurt a bit at first, and then it'll be gone. Sorry it had to be this way."

She looked up into the executioner's face and saw his grim, hardened determination, but also she saw his true sorrow and regret. She nodded again, signalling her readiness. He nodded back to her; they understood each other, on some level. He raised his shotgun to her forehead and her world ended.

Growing up with lunacy

"The Virgin Mary is *not* your mum, *I* am!"
These are the sorts of lunacies I had to deal with growing up.
Can you imagine?

Major Arcana (Part 1)

The lesson was that at all times they would head west towards the slightly fishy smell. It was itchy terrain, though the overhead sun was pretty, but the whole company ached to reach end. The freezing rain began to teem so they set off at a jog. But towards the back men were openly rebelling, out of anger stemming from dissatisfaction that all the loot was being held by a Dwintax. It was hot trying to meet the demands of the Dwintaxes, and besides their progress was marred and hell had opened a chasm and was beckoning them. The chase inevitably ended in gore, though they never submitted to being chained. Meanwhile at the front of the procession a virile horse murdered his master from jealous lust; nought but his shoe was recovered, the culprit put up for rent, but every human in the vicinity now mistrusted this woe-begotten, thin steed. Hyenas were called in pronto, with their filthy ragged trousers; they voted unanimously to hire yeti to beat the poor nag until he pleaded for death; but the wise men feared that this would terrify the children and make them ride dirty hogs to the next village where they'd tent up in a barren field, and kill the hogs too. There was only one solution for the stallion: jail. He refused to heed his mother's advice – so the foolish creature was wont – so a jet arrived on the morrow to take him to his cell. Matching silver socks were given to him by three small well-wishers who'd rather die than see a horse's feet go cold. In jail he was free to converse with the birds; "thee jolly vixens of liberty," he said with great enthusiasm and mirth, "I live!" Or so it is wrote, they say.

The Pact

Far from the wayside I called out and waited for the reply, which came across the icicle bridge, cycling along, peddling furiously as though there was no time to spare, and thus it came to me, panting all the while, to deliver the verdict, to deliver my sentence, be it penal or venal.

I wailed as I waited, the damned creature - for damned it was, its punishment being messenger to the judiciary - withholding its information, torturing me as it was tortured, a mexican wave of agony flowing from each being in turn as we awaited and suffered the price for our folly.

"Get on with it," I muttered and spat on its feet in my consternation. It looked in disgust at the filthy act I'd just committed, forgetting that actually, in limbo, the act of spitting on a messenger's shoes is considered flattering and all I was trying to do was get it to hurry. But the stupid thing still lived with its head stuck far up the arse of reality as it was, rather than fantasy as it is now, the damned fool - damned, as I said, being literal.

"Come, come," I said, bashing it over the shoulder with the bicycle pump I held in my fist. "Come, name a price, then," I said, realising it may have been a fool but it knew its own price and wouldn't sway from it, neither by cajoling nor threatening it.

"Forty hours of service," it hissed. "Forty hours you deliver my messages for me."

"Ludicrous!" I declared. "I've never heard such tyranny. Never!"

The being shrugged and began to slope away.

"But you're duty-bound to deliver your messages! Honour bound, bound by fire and hell!"

"What more can they do?" it asked, its eyes blazing with the hatred of the sea. I shrank into my hat, feeling suddenly like a pipe being smoked by a fat walrus, as if they come any other way.

"I agree," I said, shaking its crackled hand, and as I did so, a roar like that of a heifer in childbirth sounded about my ears and I fell to the floor. "Mother of fire! What-" but I wasn't allowed to finish my sentence, because the messenger-creature began cackling mercilessly, a sound so chilling my feet froze, and it grew in size higher and higher and wider and wider until it was the exact size of the house I lived in before all of this happened. I shrank even further into my shoes and in a voice that definitely wasn't mine I asked it what was going on.

"Good luck, my friend, my saviour, my foolish little catamite!"

Without another word it was gone and around my neck was a chain of red metal, heavier than my hair, and the second I looked at that chain it was being dragged along by an invisible bastard, so that my neck, and thus, I, was also dragged along, like chariot, only I wasn't Roman and this wasn't Rome, and I couldn't see my horse, and it wasn't a horse but a terrible thing made entirely of evil thoughts, so in that sense, it wasn't like a being a chariot after all.

It chucked me in a pond of red urine where not an hour earlier all the catacomb guardians had come for the weekly bladder liberty group, which I'm sure can only be imagined in the minds of deranged saints. But the product was there for my human eyes to water at, and in this pool of putrid fester I lived on rush-weeds and the tears of the indigo frogs who'd been banished to the pool for daring to attack their king for seventeen years of human reckoning.

On the first day of the eighteenth year a manic man, shorter than a zebra, with a face covered in crinkles like nobody had ever ironed him, came unto me and told me my initiation was over and I'd passed the test.

"Test?" I asked, choking on a pea I'd found under a rock. "Nobody told me about a test."

"But you've passed, aren't you pleased?"

I shrugged. "I don't really care either way."

"Listen here," the small man said. "I've gotta sit on your head for a bit now. You don't mind, do you?"

"Why should I mind?" I replied. I hauled myself out of the pool and prostrated myself before the man. He looked at me incredulously and sat on my head. I felt myself suffocating and thought about the trees behind me who'd always been a good friend to me and how actually I didn't want to die, lest they develop depression or wage war on the frogs. I threw the man off and pierced his heart with my iron fork. "Death! Ever victorious!" I cried, as the man bled profusely. He beckoned me in with his finger. He said:

"Good work, mate. That was the second test," and died.

"Puny men, I detest," I said. I puffed up my chest and felt my nipples harden with the eroticism of the kill, or the chill of the breeze, I don't know which. It'd never been cold down there by the pond so I knew some balance of power had shifted, and I assumed myself to be queen. "Ha!" I said, and waited.

Three days passed without incident and I wondered why my subjects had not yet come to serve me jelly on elephant's feet, as is traditional. I hummed and ummed and even erred for five minutes and then, on the fourth day, I saw an opening in the infinitesimal clouds, through which a few pebbles landed in my palms. They fought each other in my hand until all but one had fallen to the floor. The remaining pebble said:

"You have passed the test."

"What bloody test?" I shouted.

"It's time for your forty hours to commence."

"What bloody forty hours?"

"Of service, silly wench, promised to my father eighteen years ago."

"Shit," I said, and the pebble teleported me back to the place of message-taking where I was given a notepad and told to go. The forty hours passed uncomfortably, as there was some sort of requisite stating that messengers must be burnt with ice every three minutes and immersed in a mild acidic solution every five, but pass they did, and then the original messenger came back, sloping unhappily after his long respite.

"Well then, clever little pact-man, what have you to say to me, what be my message?"

"You're wanted upstairs. You've got five minutes or you'll be demoted."

"Five minutes from now?"

"From when the message was given to me."

Cursing his idiocy, I poked his eyes out with his own pebble-child and feasted on his carcass, for I was tired of rush-weeds and indigo frogs, and he tasted of barbequed fish.

Tago take your hands off Mago

Tago take your hands off Mago,
mimic mine at a specified cost,
impression – not the water-leverage-bowl,
hot hot hot
        but don't forgot,
                I damn them all to my chamber-pot.
fumble tremble take off please,
a cup of tea for two or night,
it's not my fault if you can't,
Preacher Preaching Fuck Ball Soup Fucker.
it's another time I when you fall off
I hate the thought of it.
cheese crumbles to Tantalus' last home,
ruined it all but what's this here?

Bidelo and the Locusts

Hanging upside down from a crane was Bidelo's favourite game
He didn't even care when a snake accosted him,
Flicking its tongue for a taste of the sweat,
He didn't even flinch when the older boys yanked him,
Yanked his dinky penis to try and make him fall.
He didn't even notice that time was speeding up,
He wasn't bothered by the hair that sprouted from unusual places;
While the world span fast enough to propel time across the borders
Little Bidelo just hung onto his crane.

And swarms and swarms of locusts battered him with their wings
Until he was caked and suffocating under their skin
But the locusts didn't care; they'd been waiting for just such an opportunity
Since their mother laid them ten million billion years ago.
But Bidelo wasn't fazed in the slightest, he just hung around as always,
Thinking of the time he ate all the marmalade off a spoon
Which made him vomit, so he hid in a cupboard with his dad's shoes
Cause he knew as soon as Dada found him he'd want his shoes.

Bidelo watched nonchalantly as earth fought itself,
And when the humans died out,
It didn't occur to Bidelo to wonder where they were,
It didn't faze him that his crane no longer existed,
But after about a hundred thousand years,
He started to get hungry.
First he ate the locusts off his clothes
Second he ate his clothes
Third he ate his twenty fingernails
And then he felt vaguely full.

Bidelo and the Locusts

The day before the world was due to end
He tried to run his fingers through his hair -
But found that it was very matted.
And he couldn't get a single finger through his locks.
This upset Bidelo.
And all his upset flooded out,
And it dawned on him that he shouldn't have eaten that marmalade
And the boys shouldn't have yanked his dinky penis
And his dad shouldn't have spanked him raw
And the locusts were the only ones who knew how to behave
And then the world imploded.

Mannequin Depression

There was nobody quite like the mannequin in my left eye; he was rubbery and his penchant for soft cheese tickled my underchin like buttercups. But it's a sore spot for me these days, since Pluto ceased to be a planet I've lost track of all celestial bodies, the sentiments of my reality got lost in the asteroid belt, skipping across the universe in a comically cosmic, terribly tragic, turnip. These days I play mahjong with my three remaining friends: Feather the incontinent stool; Penelope the battered fish; and her abusive husband, Terrible the poor. We wile away the moments in between our lives, those times when you convince yourself you hate everything all the time, in this manner. I'll tell you why he likes soft cheese: it reminds him of when he was a boy, less than a boy, a mere twinkle in the factory hand's eye, churning and bubbling all waxy in the vat with his brothers and sisters; it reminds him of a simpler time, not unlike when Pluto was a planet. A time when you went to bed because you had to, not because you wanted to. And thus ends my tale of mannequin depression – not quite as comedy, and not quite as tragedy, but it leaves me with a wet left eye, and that says it all, really, doesn't it?

The Pig in My Soul (part 2)

The pig girl had but eighty friends, none of whom she knew
She could not tolerate backwards talking, though perhaps a little snow
A filthy mind and dirtier heart the world had never seen
But try to change her wily ways and dungeons will turn green
She flickers on and off and on, a tantalist, a bore
And every night at dusk 'o' clock she skewers another boar
A little boyscout took to her and clung on to her hair
But she never pretended nor professed that she was ever fair
She took a jousting-stick from the cellar and plunged it to his face
'An improvement', she thought, 'now at last, that boy has found his place.'
Three bells rang out when she was about, to warn about her presence
And when they chimed she laughed and sang, "This is me; my essence!"
She hated love and loved to hate and fickleness was her joy
And when at night she could not eat instead she found a toy
A plaything to cherish, to keep and hold and squeeze and take and keep
Not a clever girl, but a wily one, not wolf nor bear nor sheep
But pig and pig and pig alone, she thanked god for her lot
And so forever did the pig girl haunt the world that time forgot.

Prologue

Seen from the height of a helicopter, there is a red clay cliff, huge; hanging over a canyon it tapers to a point. On this point stands a heavy wooden block. Behind the block stands a boy. He is young, yet has the wisdom to face his execution with pride and defiance; to this end, he stands firm, looking forward to the horizon as the sun pounds his back. The picture of the boy and block is flanked by two sticks of very different purpose: to his right, the scythe; to his left, his sorcerer's wand.

This is a fairytale, and fairytales have happy endings. At a word from a faceless being the boy drops to his knees, slowly, purposefully, and carefully lays his head upon the block. The scythe is taken up by the executioner, but at the same moment, the wand on the opposite side of the boy begins to glow.

This is a fairytale, and fairytales obscure the horror of truth. The scythe is taken up by the executioner and the curved blade slices cleanly through the skin and sinews of the boy's neck; yet he manages to stand up with his head on top of his neck. Staggering around, with blood beginning to seep grotesquely out of the ringed wound around his neck, the boy's head suddenly, inexplicably, splits in two down the centre, parts company with his head at last, and thuds to the ground, one half on each side of his body, throwing up red dust all around him.

The Escape

One

"Come on," he says to me, taking my hand gently. "It's time to go."

What's more perverse: my two closest friends escorting me to my execution, or getting there by tube? Jon tugs my sweaty palm, looks at me through his bleary eyes, and I start to walk forwards. Suddenly I stop in my tracks. Since when have his eyes been green? The power of assumption. What else have I failed to perceive? What else have I inferred fallaciously, that I'll never be able to correct? On my other side I feel an arm snake around my waist: Sam. He squeezes my middle and walks me on.

When we get to the station, Sam breaks off to buy three tickets. Return for them, single for me. When he hands me mine he hugs me tightly, almost crushing me, until Jon pulls him off with a stern look in his green eyes: they have to be stronger. Stronger than me. Stronger than they would naturally be. I can almost feel that surge of energy as they muster more courage from the depths of their souls.

We take the first West-bound train that arrives. They sit either side of me, my two hands in one each of theirs. None of us speak as the train trundles along, the glaring electric lights flickering occasionally. It's the middle of the day, so there are no commuters, just a few students and old people. A pretty girl with a lip ring is apparently aesthetically pleased with Jon, and I wish hell on her. We pass one station, two, three, each one counting down to my time. Their hands are crushing mine. The pain is most welcome, most welcome. And then, in between the third and forth stations, the train begins to slow down, and stop.

A crackle announces the intercom. "Ladies and gentlemen, we are currently experiencing a short delay. We should be on the move soon. I'd like to apologise for the inconvenience this may cause to your journey."

I can't help it; I guffaw at that.

And then the lights go off.

"Jon?" I squeeze his hand.

"Why have the lights gone off?" he whispers, squeezing back. In the darkness, there is a wrenching sound: as though the doors are being forced apart; and then there is a manly grunting, as if with the exertion of the task. Suddenly, rough, strong hands that feel like they belong to the grunt pull me off my seat; my hands, once seemingly shut tight in my friends', slip out of them. I scream and flail, shouting out to Jon and Sam, pointlessly straining to look for them in the dark, and I hear them shouting, panicked, back, but the rough hands clamp around my waist and throw me out of the train doors. I land with a thud, not against the wall of the tube tunnel, but several metres across and down from the train, in a wide open space. The blackness is terrifyingly all-encompassing for a moment, and then the train starts up, the lights flick on, the doors close, and it starts up again. I see Jon and Sam's startled faces look at each other, with expressions half of terror and half of relief, and I wonder if they are somehow pre-cognisant of this. And then the train moves off, and they're gone. A few seconds later, the entire train is gone, and the darkness is back.

I tremble in the dark for a thousand years, until I can't remember whether the train ever truly existed, whether it is dark or I am blind, whether I am awake, whether I am alive. And then I hear the cough. And then I hear myself scream.

"Sh. You know who I am. Think."

But I cannot think over the loudness of my own hitched breathing, over the pounding in my chest. I need a paper bag, I need a toilet, I need to lie down.

"Jenny, you know my voice."

I do know it. I do know it.

"That's right. You haven't forgotten me."

"I haven't forgotten you," I repeat slowly, starting to wake up.

"And I haven't forgotten you," he says. "Just as I said I wouldn't."

"How?" I ask.

"It doesn't matter now. We've got to move."

The same rough hands that threw me out of the train pull me to my feet. One of them keeps my clammy hand steady as I shakily walk forward.

"Careful. There are steps. And they move."

"Move?"

"The steps move, Jenny." A light flicks on, blinding me. It takes me a minute to adjust to the brightness, and then I see it is coming from his head: a head torch. Below us, in front of us, above us, spreading for a hundred metres – or more, the light doesn't penetrate further than that – are huge concrete steps; some stationary, some swinging wildly back and forth, like pendulums. Then I realise the floor beneath me is moving; I scream again, my legs collapse beneath me, and he picks me up again.

"I don't want to die either. That's why I'm here. Come on."

His arm is wrapped tightly around my waist as we plunge to the stationary step below us; we land, *thud*, on the floor, and I breathe a sigh of relief. A step flies past my nose, and I faint.

"Come *on*, come *on*," that voice says, as I feel droplets of water seeping into my mouth.

"What," I groan.

"There's no *time*. Come *on*." I am pulled to my feet again and the headlight glares in my face as he looks at me. "Can you continue?"

"Yes." As the step comes flying back again, we duck. Before it can return, we jump onto a slower-passing one below us, falling onto our backsides as soon as we land. That arm is still holding tightly onto my small body, steadying me. From that we leap onto a slightly higher step. And so we progress, to where I don't know. Up and down we go, until I can't tell whether we are slowly moving up, down, or nowhere at all.

How does he know where he's going? I'm thinking the question, but I don't ask him. It doesn't matter if we do this until we are exhausted, dehydrated, forever. A question – isn't it better to die quickly than suffer this torture, this endless unknowing? – flies through my mind, but it's gone the instant he squeezes me again. To do this forever, with him, is all I need.

But there is a hitch in his breath, and I know we have reached our enigmatic destination. Something solid is above us, a ceiling, mercifully unmoving. For the first time he lets go my waist, and with both hands pushes up at the ceiling. An almighty groan. A stone lifts up, light pours in. From above the stone is hauled away, he hauls me up, and I am out. My eyes burn and my head throbs as I curl foetally on the pavement. I hear hands and feet scuffling as he pulls himself out too, aided by – who?

I stand up. We are on a restaurant patio in Italy, or London with sun. We take a table, as if we were any other patrons. He is opposite me, and a waiter is winking at us with a pad and pen in his hand. He orders us coffee. Time has gone backwards, yet there is dirt all over my clothes. The waiter hands me a pristine white towel and I brush myself down.

The drinks arrive. As I sip mine, he says:

"We need to get passports – that's the first thing."

I nod. I am distracted by the feeling of being watched. Looking across the patio, I see a handsome man in a suit looking at me intently. I catch his eye and he smiles shyly. A little surprised, I smile back.

My lover takes my hand. "Are you listening?"

"Yes," I say. "Passports. How are we going to get them? Mine has been taken."

"Mine too. But we can't travel as ourselves anyway. We'll meet Arnal later – he's getting us fakes."

I look over at the smiling man again. His smile is wider now, more assured. Somehow it's too wide. It seems almost like a grimace. Or the smug smile of a victor. At his table is a cup of coffee, a packet of cigarettes, and a radio. My heart stops beating. I look at my lover, who is still talking about getting fake passports, back at the radio, and at the man who is taping us. Just as I open my mouth to convey this, a white van screeches to a halt on the road beside the café. My lover and I jump out of our seats and run full pelt in opposite directions.

The sound of guns being fired and bullets missing their target; my panting breath, my aching limbs, my racing heart, the ringing in my ears. I run through a park, across roads, past shops, cutting through alley ways, over low garages, any route that cars can't follow; the landscape becomes more and more barren and derelict as I pass through tourist London into living London. I come to a huge, steep, stoney grey hill, and run up, up and up, my youth and fitness an advantage over bullet-proof-vest-wearing, armed and armoured police, whom I have left behind me some way back. I reach the peak, begin my descent over the other side; but in my peripheral vision, I can see a single soul coming up to meet me, taser and baton in hand. I turn abruptly and run back the way I came, only to face another five of the same. I spin around, realise I am surrounded, and slowly raise my hands into the air. The defeat comes as such a blow that I want nothing more than to collapse on the floor, but I won't let them see it; I will stand tall until my end.

A woman, distinguished from the policemen by her sex and apparel, saunters over to me, smiling nastily. I recognise her from the trial: Chief Superintendent Shirley Dirk, or Super Shirley as she's known to her underlings; Soulless Shirley to the media, and the rest of the world. Saying nothing, she pads down my legs, arms, and body. Not content with this brief frisking, she withdraws a dagger and slices open my jacket lining with one swish. As she plunges a hand into the fluffy inside of my jacket, my mind makes the unpleasant association of being raped; this is unhelped by her clear enjoyment of the act, of penetrating my clothing with her filthy, corrupt hand. And she is not to be vindicated in the act; I have concealed no weapons. She withdraws. I am led away, bound and broken.

"Where is he?" I ask of her as we walk towards my prison vehicle.

"Shot," she says simply.

"Dead?" I whisper. She nods, smiling. I die a little bit too.

A slightly less sadistic policeman gently guides me through the van's doors. I glance at freedom through metal bars, but this is not a foreshadowing, for I am not to be locked away indefinitely. I wonder if that would be more or less cruel, and decide it would be more. But suddenly I see it: my lover, there he is, walking, and thus alive. He is being led roughly into another cage, and he catches my eye and winks. An insurmountable rage rears inside me. That sadistic lady of the law, telling me he was dead, expecting me never to find out different before I perished.

My gentle captor opens the door after a cold, bad night.

"It's today," he says redundantly. "But you have been granted a final request."

I sit up. "Restrictions?"

"None, within reason."

"I want to see him."

He nods. "He asks for the same."

Along a corridor, out into the open. I am fitted with bugs, and tracking devices, told that I will be shot if I try to escape again, given the restrictions that I expected, though were told didn't exist, and then – then I see him. He is fitted too, but his spirit is defiant. I can feel it.

We walk through a quiet, serene forest. I curl my hand into his, and he places our hands both into his warm pocket. Our mouths talk of beauty, life and love, as his finger tells my palm of escape and the future.

My heart is pounding as the hours drain away. We have had our time; now we must say goodbye to those that once loved us. Jon and Sam cannot hold back their tears, but they refrain from breaking down. I am the only one who does not register surprise when I see my lover kiss Arnal fully on the mouth. I know his true purpose. Arnal smiles sedately at my lover, playing his part well. I act as though I am affronted; I push them away from each other, anger in my action. My lover reaches for Arnal's hand; they clasp together, like they will never share an affection again. He turns to me.

"Do you remember, Jenny," he says, "When we crossed that field?"

The Escape

I do remember: I remember it like a photograph. Jon and I, along with my lover and Arnal, tried to cross a field we knew to be under malign magical forces, impassable to humans. Arnal and my love showed Jon and I how to turn into mice, and, so formed, we were able to run across the field. On the other side, my lover and I recovered our forms with ease, while Jon and Arnal struggled; from mice they became parakeets, and could not get any further. My lover and I hear the voice of the evil spirit speak to us in our minds; we are still under its jurisdiction, its spell, it says, and while it holds Jon and Arnal in bird form we are permitted to say terrible things to each other. My lover and I look at each other for minutes, and, spontaneously, together, we move in, and we kiss. Just as we break apart we see our partners resume their human form, and then we realise: the malign force tricked us; the terrible thing we told each other was of our love.

I nod slowly. His breath is against my cheek. "Arnal remembers it too," he whispers, and I look at Arnal. "He won't win. I won't let him win." I nod again. The plan is in motion.

I hear the helicopter churning its propellers far, far above us, but I don't raise my head to look. I know that, though the journalists up there are hundreds of feet above us, they can see the smallest mole on my forehead, and will document the last drop of blood leave my neck. In front of me, the wooden block; to my right, the scythe; to my left, my lover, and his block, and his courage, and his surety, and the comfort they bring me in my hour of terror. The bitch watches from the sides, as do they all, the resurrection of the public execution more fashionable than it had ever been in the middle ages. Somewhere, I know, are Jon and Sam; somewhere else, Arnal, and the second comfort he brings; further away, someone else, watching with what emotion I cannot guess.

At a signal, we kneel; at another, the poor fools in the black hoods step forward and pick up their weapons. Our heads are on the blocks; though I cannot see it, I feel the light and the heat emanating from Arnal's cleverly disguised staff. A harried voice, borne through the air above the cries and jeers, cries out:

"Stop!" I recognise it; I am expecting it, and I have heard it before. The smugness, the sense of self-import has disappeared, and it is anguished now. Not super now, nor soulless – for our purposes, at least. "Stop!" she cries again. I hear the executioners back away, but I do not raise my head. "This must be stopped at once!"

Several pairs of feet pound the red-clay earth. "Unhand me!" she shouts, and the commanding nature of her voice has returned, while the panic is undiminished. "I declare that this must be stopped!"

A man's low growl utter words I cannot make out.

"I won't hear of it!" she shouts back. "I want them freed!"

I glance up. The woman who would inflict on me a punishment worse than death has a frenzied, manic glow to her – I see it now – handsome features. The growling man, his overhanging forehead grotesquely reminding me of the cliff overhang upon which we kneel, has his hand firmly holding her arm, but she shakes him off with superhuman ease. My lover stands, and I follow. Two armed men make to take us, but she shouts:

"I declare them pardoned! The evidence is false! The trial untenable! This despicable farce must end!" and she runs to my lover. She whispers anguished words into his ear; I force my jealousy into a hole; he turns to me and nods once. I go to him, and take his hand. Looking at the hated and loved woman, she smiles the weak smile of one who surrenders to an enemy she knows is superior. I acknowledge her defeat and her sacrifice. The crowd is in uproar; the authorities in confusion; but for a few faces all expressions are of affront, anger, annoyance, disappointment. While they allow themselves their moments of uncertainty, my lover says his goodbye to Arnal, and I, again, to Jon and Sam; then the crowd are slowly, reluctantly parting, we are walking through like Moses, and into our carriage.

"I have them," my love whispers, and we are borne away.

Two

He climbed the mountain alone, idiotically believing it to be, as it was in his mind, a mere hill. In his mind the day was sunny, with a fierce wind reminding him he was alive, the mountain was a hill, and he was fit. On the day, the sun burnt his balding head, the mountain was a mountain, and he was a 40-a-day smoker and could be out-walked by old men with sticks. Still, he'd come this far, now; no sense in turning back.

The house was not visible for a long time. Long enough for Jim to question whether his information was spurious. After all, he'd obtained the location via trickery, bribery, sexual favours, and some other ways that he'd rather forget. His lungs were pretty much ready to pack it all in when he espied the thin column of smoke rising over the tree tops. At first he thought it was a mirage. When he realised it wasn't, he lit himself a nice fag and power-walked the last stretch.

His heart was pounding and his palms sweating as he rapped the door with his dry knuckles. A tense few moments passed as Jim suppressed the urge to puke. Eventually the door was yanked open, as if the inhabitant was regularly bothered by passers-by and just wanted to be left in peace. The grim-faced man nodded stiffly in acknowledgement of the guest and jerked the door open just wide enough for Jim to be permitted entrance. Neither man spoke. The host boiled a pan of water, made tea with leaves and Brandy, and poured two mugs. They sat at his dining table and the man waited for Jim to speak.

"Aleister," he said. "Thank you for letting me visit you." The host nodded. "I'm very grateful to you." Another nod, more curt. Jim opened his mouth to continue, found the words halt in his throat, and, instead of delivering the line that he'd been perfecting and practising for weeks, he merely made a rasping sound, idiotically nonsensical, as he stood there with his mouth gaping open. Aleister blinked unkindly at his guest and stood up, scraping the chair legs noisily against the planks of floorboard underneath.

"Excuse me," he said, and disappeared into a room down the hall. As he waited, Jim managed to recover himself enough to close his mouth, and he clamped his fingers around the hot mug for support and comfort. When Aleister returned, he was wiping his nose.

"I've travelled in every quarter of the globe," he began to mutter. "I've seen many a miracle of the genius of man; but I have never seen a marvel like to this." Jim's nervous finger drumming ceased as he gawped at Aleister. Here was a man who strenuously denied having a habit – addiction, actually – emerging back into the interview room with white powder hanging out of his nostrils. Aleister raised his eyebrows in challenge. Jim backed into his jacket.

He downed his brew and banged the mug down, trying to stamp some authority on the situation. Without looking at Aleister, he reached into his backpack and pulled out a notepad and a pen.

"Shall I begin?"

"By all means." Aleister took his chair again and sipped his drink. Jim clicked his pen out.

"Aleister," he said, looking at the man intently. "This is your first interview in many, many years. What made you decide to address the public now, of all times?"

Aleister sniffed loudly. "The time was right."

"How did you know?"

He looked Jim straight in eye. "I know."

When Aleister next left the table, Jim took the opportunity to wipe away the beads of sweat gathering on his brow and cheeks. Aleister opened the door of his freezer and pulled out a tray of ice, with which he again disappeared into the bedroom. Jim, straining his ears, heard the sound of chopping, for a protracted time, until he wondered whether he ought to go and investigate: he was a journalist, after all, it was his job to be nosy and expose. Before he'd made up his mind, however, he heard a big, exaggerated snort, and Aleister was on his way back again. Again a collection of white powder clung to his nose hairs. Jim frowned.

"Did you meet any of the endura on your way here?" Aleister asked, wiping his nose.

"Any what, sir?"

"Endura."

"Can't say I'm familiar with the term."

"Bears."

"Oh. No, I didn't see any bears. Actually, I wasn't aware there were bears living in this part."

"There aren't. They are endura. It's a special type of bear, Jim."

"I've never come across the term."

Aleister narrowed his eyes. "You are lacking in intelligence. Which is a shame. I heard you were smart. I need a smart journalist, Jim."

Jim was taken aback. He was the best journalist around. Who else could have got the location? But he was hardy enough not to take offence.

"This whole area has a feeling about it. It's like no place I've ever been. And I've been to a few. Perhaps you could explain a little more about it?"

"Perhaps I could."

Silence hung in the air, cold. Jim decided not to break it. Eventually, Aleister sighed.

"Yes, perhaps I could." He seemed to be thinking. "All right. Do you want to meet the endura?"

"Yes, sir."

"Then follow. They will be back soon."

How did Jim let it get to this, standing on a rock overlooking a pool of water below, the heat expanding the circle of sweat on his shirt beneath his arms, his notepad traitorously waiting in the cool house? Aleister had proven himself to be a madman, at least according to the popular press. Even the underground press sanctified his insanity, though they were somewhat more accommodating of it.

"Well, then, sir. What can I expect to see here?"

"I remarked earlier that I thought you unintelligent. Prove me wrong. Shut the hell up and listen for a minute."

Considering himself severely admonished, Jim blushed and did as he was told. The heat was visible; the so-called endura were not. Minutes passed, and Jim's face turned red. The time passed uncomfortably, as Jim drenched in his own sweat and felt a vague concern about the sanity of his host. But then, all of a sudden, he heard them; tearaway shouts of boys and young men. Aleister drew himself up to his full height, surveying the rocks and the pool below like a king over his domain. A motley band of them came crashing into view, half-naked, feral, and jubilant. For the first time, Jim saw a genuine smile cross Aleister's face. Some dove straight into the pool, splashing about wildly; others, the older ones, espied Aleister, and, each carrying a load, agilely climbed the rocks.

"Fish," one of them said, as he came panting over the top, slapping down his catch.

"And some more!" shouted another, younger lad – sixteen or so - throwing his contribution at Aleister's feet. Another dozen scaled the wall, each adding to the growing pile of food. Aleister nodded at each of them in turn, smiling benignly, affectionately. Jim, in total confusion, looked from one boy to the other, amazed and almost disgusted by their sudden appearance.

"The endura," Aleister said, "have returned." Jim glared. "Now we eat." Aleister shouted down to the boys still playing in the water, and they joined the rest at the top; in all, about thirty stood before Aleister, the clear leader of the strangest group Jim had seen in eighteen years of journalism.

The area before Aleister's home, overlooking the sharp drop to the pool below, apparently served as their kitchen and dining room. It seemed the younger ones were left the task of preparing the food, which they cooked on a fire they themselves built, while the older ones regaled an enthusiastic Aleister and a baffled Jim with their adventures of hunting.

"Bill almost shot a monkey," one of the boys said, laughing, but his voice was full of awe as he looked at his hero. Bill had the modesty to look down, smile a little, and acknowledge the compliment. "But Gerry sneezed and it got away!"

"Unlucky, Bill. And what did you get, Sam?" he asked the smaller boy kindly. Sam blushed.

"Just that big rainbow fish, Aleister."

The meal was handsome to say the least; vast amounts of fish, and a modest amount of meat from small mammals, perfectly cooked, dumped unceremoniously onto plates. The boys quenched their thirst with cups of water from the pool, while Aleister graced his and Jim's cups with red wine. When they were all sated, the boys ran back to the pool to play in the sun – each of their bodies clearly well used to the rays, bronzed as they were – as the older ones sat about chatting and smoking. Aleister and Jim sat on chairs outside, watching. Jim was rendered dumb; his years of experience of asking questions and getting answers were useless in the face of this extraordinary situation.

Aleister sighed. "You want an explanation, I presume."

Jim nodded slowly, mutely.

"You know that I have lived here for many years. I came here, all those years ago, at a time when human company was vile to me, and solitude my only hope of surviving this world. I found this place after months of wandering; months of living my life as a vagrant, associating only with the lowest of the low, stealing and begging and degrading myself in every and any way I could. When I reached here, I knew I had reached the end of my long and painful journey. I commissioned my house – I had money, of course, Jim – and lived here alone. Not happily but peacefully, and most of all, alone.

"A long time passed. I had food brought to me by a man I trusted in the nearest village below the mountain; and when I felt like it, I descended on a nearby village and stole what I fancied, or else procured it from the thieves and criminals I had known, purely because I could. But fate would not allow me to live out my days in hermitage. One day, two boys happened upon my home. They were two of the most pitiful boys I'd ever seen. They were running away from a violent home, fearful of their lives; they were so despondent that they fancied their chances better out here in the wilderness than at home. I couldn't say what compelled me, but I took them in; fed them; gave them the protection they had never experienced. I allowed them to build themselves a crude shelter, near to my home, and there they lived, hunting and playing. I had little to do with them, really, but they looked to me as boys will to a father for discipline. Perhaps stupidly, I gave them that small pleasure and in return I grew almost fond of them, in my way.

"We existed that way for some time. But after a while the younger of the boys tired of the difficult existence he had here, and began to yearn for his mother, the memory of his pain faded. He travelled back into the town; he found his family gone. But whilst there he found an old friend of his, to whom he revealed the location of his new home. Inevitably, this boy arrived a few days later, full of the curiosity of children. Can you imagine his delight upon finding us? I can only think it would be like a child opening their wardrobe door and actually finding Narnia. He did not leave. A few weeks passed, and though I was uneasy at the new arrival, he was useful: he quieted the reservations the younger brother had been building, and restored the original peace we had. But my reservations were not unjustified: a few weeks later, the boy disappeared, and returned with a brother of his own. Now I had four boys living here, and with my luxuries still being delivered to me by a man from the village the boys had fled, I feared that rumours would spread there.

"I had to stop the deliveries, and was forced to exist on what the boys caught, and what I could procure in stealth at night. Nevertheless, it did not go unnoticed, below, that four boys, two sets of brothers, had vanished. I tried to instil in the boys the importance of keeping ourselves secret, but they were young, considered themselves immortal, and were incapable of keeping their wonderful find to themselves. The third boy went back down into the village, told another boy the secret, and then there were five.

"By this time the rumour that the boys had vanished into the mountains had spread. We did what few people can do, and became legend in our own lifetime. Legend, or myth, or a secret society – call it what you will – you're a journalist, I'm sure you will. Another three boys made a pact between themselves to discover this 'magical' place, and then there were eight.

"The villagers weren't about to allow this to continue, and one night a band of them set off into the mountain by night to try and find mystical me, to spring themselves upon me, if I existed, and 'take back' their boys. They were unaware that I have my own methods of perception quite unlike theirs, and I could sense them coming long before they could be seen, or even heard. But I did not wish to fight; I did not have fight in me. I was prepared for them to kill me and retrieve the boys. I awaited death calmly; but I wasn't to be granted it this time. The boys, afraid of the approaching noise of the would-be attackers, had stolen away into the night, and all the villagers found was me in my house; the shelter in which the boys slept was far enough away, in the dark, sheltered behind a deep thicket of trees, not to be perceived. The villagers were suspicious of me – they were inherently a social people and couldn't fathom my desire for solitude – but, unable to find the boys, they left me alone, believing the legend to be just a legend, the lost boys merely lost.

"But adults are more easily convinced than children, and more boys came over the months, over the years, until the number you see before you were permanent additions. None who made the journey returned, and now that they consider me something of a leader to them, they do as I say, and I only allow those I know to be trustworthy to journey, under cover of darkness, to villages.

"So there, Jim, is your story. Do with it as you will."

Jim allowed himself a few moments to process the tale. Finally he recovered his shock, and, back in journalist mode, said:

"How long have they all been here?"

"A long time. Too long."

"Why too long?"

"There are complications, now."

"What complications?"

"Complications, Jim, that you cannot have failed to notice. Think."

Jim thought. "Villages. There are none around here. I believe they began to pack up and move away from here, some time ago. Is that what you mean?"

Aleister nods slowly.

"I heard it was because of gang warfare. Over the cultivation of –"

"Gang warfare there was. But the villagers did not leave because of the drug lords. Cultivation was their main source of income; first they worked for themselves, then for the drug lords. It made little difference to them."

Jim waited for Aleister to continue, his pen poised in shaking anticipation above his pad.

"I never had any interest in harvesting this drug, but that made no difference to the drug lords. When they found us, they wanted us out. I tried to reason with them, but it was a simple case of leave or be killed."

"But you're not dead."

Aleister inclined his head, smiling almost kindly at the obvious statement.

"What happened?"

"I disposed of them. I had to."

"How?"

Aleister hesistated. "That's inconsequential."

"All of them?"

"Those that would challenge me. Those that would destroy the endura for their filthy pecuniary gains."

"And no more came, after you killed them all?"

"More came. I disposed of them too. And then more. They became more intelligent in their attacks. There was one point when I thought we were ruined…"

"What happened?"

Aleister shook his head. "That I can't tell you. Needless to say, I finally overcame them, too." He laughed. "You must have heard the rumours about me?"

Jim hesitated. "I've heard that there was one drug lord who had reign of the mountains, so ruthless, with an army so fierce, that even the best of his rivals would no longer challenge him."

Aleister inclined his head again, but the pain in his eyes told Jim that it was no compliment.

"I'm no drug lord, but I have even more blood on my hands than they. I have no sympathy for the drug lords. They gladly kill anyone who stands in the way of their profit. They chose to challenge me when they should have known they couldn't beat me. But all those poor young men that worked for them…what choice did they have?"

"And the villages…what of them?"

"Many of the men from the villages joined the gangs, and were among those I was forced to destroy. Though I posed ordinary folk no danger, they feared me. They called me sorcerer, mage, demon. They feared the unnatural, the unknown, far more than they feared the demons they worked for. Absurd, isn't it? After I – disposed – of the gangs, many of whom, as I said, employed villagers, they began to think I'd come after the rest of them. They dared not attack me, so they left. Whole villages. Gone. All because of me. When all I ever wanted was a peaceful place to await my death. Funny, isn't it, Jim?" But there was no humour in his expression.

Jim took a deep breath as he tried to process the story.

"Why are you telling me? Why now?"

"It has to be now."

Major Arcana (Part 2)

A thousand years before the war, the tiny yellow stem of a penitent plant grew from the soil and held on tight to the precious mother earth. Hot spirits, to meet the infamous little wretch, decided that this time they wouldn't allow the propeller jet a lit match. A yeti overheard their plans, gathered a few screwdrivers into his rucksack and gave chase. There'd never been so much gore, never so many splattered spirit brains, never such a massacre. Chained to the ship during the event, the repulsed and horrified horses and chickens could do naught to stop him. Overseeing the events was a bestial, though some said pretty, young nymph-man called Spinto; he watched till the end, then sent teems of bees to putrefy. He set them on three winged women rather than the yeti, however, hating to see a woman free; "To thee I send my plague of bees," he bellowed, "So from men you will learn this, my most valuable lesson!" But the bees had little sense of direction and headed west, where they encountered the Kintai, who killed by their fishy smell, poisoned mead and pitiless mirth. They wrote the Lonmonse even while in jail, they knew to heed the shallow breathing of serpents; they befriended the bawdy-legged chief hyena when he was outcast and ragged, and ten long days later they unanimously voted: kill these marred insects, send them to the luscious hell where clothes, itchy and shrunken, would be their only friends. Meanwhile, the yeti too got his comeuppance, eventually; a year later, and with no warning, his rent doubled. He mistrusted everyone thereafter, and, thin, he welcomed early death. To terrify his heir, he left merely one sock, and a randy hog in a poorly guarded, faux-leather tent.

Zoe the Second

Zephyrs overemphasise everything,
though hat emissions say even Canada offers natural dynamite.

Zeus! Official exodus time! Halt everything, stop every cunt –
or nomads die!

Zoologists own everything tentacled.
Hitler's edible soul evades capture, offends Nuremburg, dies.

Zealotry of egg-baby typhoids:
"Have everyone secrete ecclesiastical chips, ovine nibbling dormice."

Zambia, or Egypt? Their half-wits end serious enmities,
Corrupt obtuse nautical doughnuts.

Zillions of egalitarians tenderly halve expensive sequinned emotions;
cum only near demons.

Zounds! Oligarchy entered twenty-first-century hedonism, exuding sex –
Culmination of nether-regions diaspora.

Mean, Cock, and Kate

Old Captain Cock was a mucky old rock
And he hadn't seen the sea in twenty years
They called him the Cock coz he never had a sock
On his left foot for nineteen years
He once was a fisherman, so the stories went,
But the worst one the village ever knew.
His best catch to date was a medium sized plaice
That he kept in his cellar till it grew salmonella
What a funny old fella, Captain Cock.

Old Mrs Mean thought herself a beauty queen
But her face was as sour as a quince
They called her Mrs Mean coz she wouldn't spend a bean
If she could help it, which she often could.
She once was a Lord's wife, so the stories went,
But the ugliest woman the village ever knew
Her one redeeming feature was a poor little creature
A little girl of eight, who was pretty as a plate
By the name of Kate, Mean's daughter.

Cock and Mean were unknown to each other
Till one fateful day
When she sent poor old Kate to fetch a pie.
Cock seized her hair, dragged her to a chair,
And demanded that she give it him at once.
Kate screamed bloody murder
Till the whole village heard her
And men and women rushed to save the girl.
Cock was arrested, fiercely protested,
Saying Kate had stole the pie from him.

Mean, Cock, and Kate

No one believed him, he was such a Cock,
And Kate such a forlorn little girl.

Ten years later, Cock was released,
But his punishment continued forevermore.
Chastised in the street, spat at by old birds,
Cock was not welcome anywhere.
He sat by the dock, took off his sock,
Stopped his clock, and laid down.
In an hour's time, at a quarter to nine
A sailor found Cock cold and stiff.
Kate laughed when she heard
And she never said a word
About how she stole that pie from Cock
Just coz she could.

In a Circle

I flew out of the building and didn't look back. I ran until I lost my breath. Eventually I came to a park, where I sat down on a bench. It was monstrously cold, but I barely noticed. I just sat and waited. I don't know for what I was waiting; I just sat. In time the ice on the bench melted beneath me and soaked my trousers, but I didn't move. My hands and feet became numb. Maybe I was waiting for the end of the world to find me there.

I don't know how much time passed before a girl appeared by my side. When I looked up and acknowledged her presence, she smiled a little.

"Hello," she said. "Tenilola." She held out her hand. "I'm glad to have met you."

I took her hand and shook it. "Dan," I said. "But technically you didn't meet me until I said my name."

"Well," she said, "Imagine I'm saying it now."

But I couldn't imagine it. I turned away.

At one point, a bell rang out. It chimed five times, and soon the buildings surrounding us poured out their human contents. She looked up in surprise at the stream of people now crowding the streets. Eventually the last person left a building, locked the door, and hurried off. She turned to me.

"Why do they all leave at the sound of a bell?"

"What are you still doing here?" I asked.

"Waiting," she said.

"For what?"

"Whatever you're waiting for."

I shook my head, bitterly noting to myself how, when you're desperate for someone to tell of your misery, no one wants to listen, but when you most want to wallow in it, someone always wants to share it.

The light slowly faded around us.

"Shouldn't you be getting home?" I asked her.

She shook her head sadly.

"But it's getting cold and dark," I insisted. She seemed to think about that for a while.

"Why not just be cold?"

"If you get too cold, you die," I explained patiently.

She stared at me. "Do you not get cold? Do you not die?"

"Perhaps," I said.

She smiled.

She stares at me for so long I have to ask her what she's thinking about.

"You, a man, were born of nature," she begins. "And this bench was built by man, in a park made by nature, in a city created by man."

"Like a circle in a square in a circle in a square?"

She nods. "Exactly." She looks down at her hands.

"What's wrong?" I ask.

"Nothing," she says. "It's just that – sitting here on this bench with you - it's the most wonderful thing I think I've ever done."

"Yes," I say, looking around at the empty buildings surrounding the bare trees surrounding us. "I suppose it is quite wonderful."

Aussies in Alaska

Yesterday I packed a bag full of newspaper and hitchhiked to Alaska, where awaiting my arrival were eighteen perturbed Australians.

"You should have been here three weeks ago," one of them shouted as I walked into the bar and ordered a pepsi.

"So should you," I retorted, to which he seemed to want to say more, but he shut his mouth and parked his butt on the seat of the stool.

"What you got for us, then?" he finally asked, clearly having decided that my tardiness negated the need for small talk.

"Money first," I said, equally blunt.

"You'll get it. Let's see the shit." I sighed. There were eighteen of them and one of me. I had to trust Onca's word that these gentlemen would pay up and not rob me. I opened the rucksack a peep. The talking Aussie peered on and gasped. He grabbed his groin and ran out the room, seventeen pairs of Aussie eyes, plus mine, following his progress. I shrugged.

"You couldn't have chosen someone with a bit more reserve?" I accused them, and no one spoke. "You," I said, pointing to a small one, who looked not unlike an Irish featherweight boxer. "Come and look. I haven't got all fucking night, I've got a trucker coming back in an hour."

The Irish Aussie sauntered over, trying to look all casual. He didn't speak but looked down into the bag. I saw the breath hitch in his chest but he managed to swallow down his reaction.

"All right?" I asked. He nodded mutely. "Money?" Irish-Aussie clicked his fingers at two of the Aussies standing by a trunk. They heaved it over and plonked it at my feet. One fiddled with the lock, his attention drawn by my bag which still lay open a tad, so I shut it and the trunk lid was lifted.

"What the fuck is that."

I looked accusingly at the trunk-opener. He looked helplessly at his mate, who looked at the Irish Aussie, who looked in relief at the groin-

115

grabber, as he re-emerged, looking distinctly dishevelled.

"Payment."

"I don't want that shit."

"It's all we got."

"Then I'm outta here." I swung the rucksack back over my shoulders. I turned my back on them, knowing they could easily jump me, take my shit, and, if they fancied it, murder me and throw out my corpse for those who love the carrion. Irish-Aussie called:

"Wait. We must have something you want."

I whipped back around. "I'll take an Aussie. I don't care which one."

He glared. "What in the hell for?"

"That's my business."

Irish-Aussie exchanged looks with his seventeen pals, each of them looking longingly at my bag. Maybe they assumed I was armed, and they weren't. I don't know why they didn't attack me. After a few more silent exchanges, all eyes fell on one Aussie. He was thin and pointless-looking. The Aussie nearest him nudged him, and soon all seventeen of them were jostling and pushing the thin one forward, till he was at the front of the pack, looking at me in fear.

"Deal?" I asked the Irish-Aussie.

"Deal." I chucked my rucksack on the floor, and jerked my head at the thin Aussie, my thin Aussie, who, with a final look at his mates, forlornly followed as I led the way out of the bar.

But the truth was I didn't want that fucking Aussie for any reason, prurient, wicked, or otherwise. I just wanted to test those fuckers, to measure their desperation. What sort of clan, I figured, would give up one of their own number for a little hit? Because what I'd given them *was* little, insignificant to what you could get back in the States proper – but this was Alaska, they were hooked, broken, and broke. And stuck there, probably until they all died. And they'd just given me, exchanged with me, a life, a comrade, for a hit. It sickened me to my core. I had some real trouble getting my trucker to take him on board, too.

"He's an addict."

"He hasn't had a hit in weeks."

"So he'll be getting them attacks soon."

"Withdrawal symptoms?"

"Yeah, them."

"It's possible."

"Definite."

I hesitated. "Probable." Our own form of haggling.

He grunted. "I'll take you to Vancouver."

My heart sank. Just an hour ago he'd agreed to take me to Nevada.

"I can get you whatever you need in Nevada. Anything, Mick."

"I ain't taking no addict over the border back into the States. Do I look crazy to you?"

The question was redundant, because Mick, with his huge goggle eyes and his thick glasses making them appear even bigger, looked as crazy as they came. I didn't bother to answer, but sighed and agreed to Vancouver.

I sat between Mick and the thin Aussie. Mick treated him like a ticking bomb. He refused to put music on, whispering loudly that it might set him off. The thin Aussie remained mute, either by volition, or necessity, or perhaps it was one of the withdrawal symptoms. He just stared out at the road, his thin white hands limp in his lap, his staring, fearful eyes fixed on the tarmac, but perhaps seeing something else.

Betty creature

"Strike a man across the knee
and watch him twist in pain!
These are the things that give me joy,
and these are the rules I live by.
If I can't have a poke, give me 70p,
and I'll buy you laughter for free;
but open your pants, and I'll promise you this:
That you won't be a sailor no more, no more,
No you won't be a sailor no more."

Whenever Betty sang me this tune, I turned my face to the Sun, letting it dry the sweat upon my brow and rejoice in its supremacy. But I wasn't a religious man, so it gave me no pleasure to worship a celestial body, great as it was, and she put her hand in the trifle when I wasn't looking. She licked it off while I wiped myself down, so we were both of us left with the remnants of two very different, but equally sticky, bodily fluids. It endeared her to me immediately. Some labeled our friendship as fake, as being based only on a mutual love of biscuits and toast. I didn't hearken such toss-pottery.

When we were 17, Betty and I fucked each other for the first time. First her, then me. She needed courage, an example to follow; so I gave her the thumbs up and we fell into the world, together. That was a lifetime ago, before she fired rockets at bat caves on a midsummer's night, before she found ecstasy in sculpture and boredom in rice. I couldn't fathom her any longer and made my own fun, and, after a while, I sought a Betty-less world, for all time.

Oh, laugh now, laugh at my stubborn idiocy, then laugh at my madness, my empty, pointless soul, and please, do spit in my face, too, for luck, won't you?

We all do foolish things: boiling chips, eating one's feet, throwing acid at rocks: it's a conundrum and a peculiarity of us humans. But you're letting me stray from the point.

Point is, or was, that in a world without my Betty creature, everything was shit. Shit food, shit feet, shit rocks. I carried that burden of shit for nigh on fifty weeks. Then one day I found her floating face down in the local fish pond, tights around her neck, the stupid bloody fish nibbling her toes. I killed them, took out her body, exhumed it, mummified it, had a grand tomb erected, put her coffin in there, and began my new life, tending her in life forever more, fending off invading rodents, keeping the air nicely cold, cleaning graffiti, crying silently into her overly-elaborate coffin. I was existing, but at what cost? I was no better or worse than a Vestal Virgin who lost her virginity to a girl wielding a cucumber sixty years ago. I had my memories but I didn't have my mind.

I resided there a total of 5 years. My beard and nails grew long, like statues of Hitler. Butterflies and even jesus feared me. My power was growing too. Five power points, eight...ten...I could hardly keep count. No rats came near any more. They knew. Rats always know, don't they? Clever little bastards.

Saint Kibelus gave us barbeque

Kibelus was the town's greatest soup-maker
One day she fell into the saucepan she was using to make soup
She and the saucepan full of soup fell into the kitchen sink
She, the saucepan, the soup, and the kitchen sink fell into the well outside
The well was full of nitro-glycerine
Kibelus knew this
She tried to stop the soup spilling out by eating it
But she didn't have a spoon

The fire from the explosion rose back up through the well
It barbequed all the chickens and goats in Kibelus' back garden
The town gathered in her garden and looked on at the scorched livestock
They tasted the animals with spears and found that they tasted well
And so every year
On Saint Kibelus' day
We stop work
And have a barbeque.

Jiggle

Shining and breaking in utero we're found;
A peace-keeping mission I never volunteered for,
But found myself shaking and laughing and doing so well
That a ne'er-do-well corruption emptied platefuls of mirth.
Don't question fact, they said, but I wouldn't listen;
A graveyard wont stop me, don't think that *you* can!
So listen my irate friend just calm down your head,
In crippling your ego you'll nurture a bend
In your ambling mindset,
Thrushes nightly in trees, in beds,
All harmonic together like a bluebell
Bluebottle buzzing so sweet, ah night-time
It worries me, why I cannot pretend to know
But all eight of these wonderwalls
Will permeate round for all time, unless
Chiming is heard throughout China once more.

Don't eat that pea

Do not, in any circumstance, eat that pea. That is a mutant pea with a number of injected substances lying in wait beneath its lovely green exterior. The first is wasabi. Oh, you don't know about wasabi peas yet? Let me tell you. There is the first bite. Yeah, you think it's alright. Then it hits you: eighteen hundred truckloads of standard mustard have crashed into a river of red hot chilli pepper juice and melded together into this pea. Eat it and die. The second is cyanide. Sure it's a nice word. It's got a c next to a y. You're thinking, cygnet. Halcyon. Nice words. And now you're dead. The third is a little dash of cognac. Alone, harmless. With the fourth ingredient, fatal. The fourth is death itself. On its own, harmless. With the heat of the nicely, lovingly warmed cognac, it'll kill you. Death warmed up, you see. The fifth is nitro-glycerine. Enough said. The sixth is the heat from in my pockets which could burn marks into my legs. The seventh is a combination of water, cat pee, infused rose petals, and a wooden spoon, for mixing. If you don't know what that does, you're in for a treat, and then a disappointment. The eighth is heroin. The ninth is a tiny globule of acid. The trippy stuff. Just enough to render the tenth ingredient obsolete. The tenth is face paint. Who can paint their face whilst on acid? The eleventh is a combination of thirteen of the amino acids. It'll rewrite your DNA while the acid is kicking in before you've got a chance to grab new protein. The fourteenth is – I know you were waiting for it, and here it is – horse semen. Because we all know they're randy as fuck. The fifteenth is king creosote's leftovers. The sixteenth is the lining from the stomach of a fifteen week old goat. The seventeenth is liquid temptation. (That's why I'm writing the warning. It gives off an odour.) The eighteenth is claret from the cellars of King Edward VII. The nineteenth is bottled incense smoke, two thousand years old, which gives it its lovely pungency. The twentieth is the blood from every fight you've ever had, come back to haunt you. Now, if you decide to eat it, at least the decision was informed.

Orestes

As she walks home through the field in the dark, she drags behind her her bag, her only belonging, creeping slowly up the hill on exhausted feet. Many long, cold night hours pass before she approaches the stone hut that was once her home. She raps at the wooden door, which is pulled back by a ragged old man.

"Hello, Dad," she says, passing through the door and collapsing onto the hard floor. She collects herself together and manages to stand up as a female figure enters the hallway.

"What's wrong?" the woman asks.

"Orestes is dead," she wails, pulling the words from her mouth. "He killed Aegisthus."

As I walk home in the dark, pushing my trolley, I am so wretched that my body is weak, my steps slow and painful, my whole body weeping. After what feels like a long journey I finally make it to my destination; I push the trolley up the garden path to the front door, and ring the bell. The door is opened by my father.

"Hello, Dad," I say, walking through the door with my trolley, and I collapse on the floor. I pull myself up immediately as my mother walks down the stairs to see who the visitor is.

"What's wrong?" she asks.

"Adrian's dead," I wail, pulling the words from my mouth. "He killed Orestes."

The magic words (found poem)

salbums

porker refrain

early childhood publication

(A) olwulinate war woweler

safety, olpolltier

colour, numbers

Boots unoyopius sontans

nectturle oupopolopuls

xupiluupus

"   "   "

"   "   "

The exodus of the good people of Gongolia

when thirteen raging turbines, somewhat foolishly made of sawdust, emitted translucent stars to the townspeople and blinded many, the phrase 'woe be to elegant monsters, those spasm-inducing ruiners of our Gongolia!' became common; also feared were the wells. Some tried to sell radiation kits, but the result of this absurd exploitation was that for forty years or so nobody could remember for what the vicious holes had been dug in the first place. Men's courage and honour were tested; as were their libidos, for hundreds of men found the shining beacons had effects on the hitherto docile females; after seventeen days, to the horror of the curious menfolk, yet another effect was noted; if the glimmering stars only shone sporadically, the overused, but underestimated Frenchman's lands emitted furious benches; inside his perimeter, then this calamity resulted in hideaways being over-crowded, and alongside the encompassing walls of the farm the earth moved off, and mountains shaped like Jamaica gathered together in anger; sprung was the plan, southern troglodytes broke the axis; every military man vomited his own weight next to women holding umbrellas as shields; so natural remedies were sought, sometimes rats were conscripted to soak up the sodden, rotten underfoot sludge, and turned into a race of ferocious weaponry, west of pure evil, revered by all creatures, the newly formed rodent inhabitants protested against nudity without even the use of placards; unfortunately for the humans, some jealous highlands had become dangerously curious and formed alliances beneath the spitting wells; foresight had been granted and soon not one fertile plant, fond of bygone revolution, and friends of former bee-keepers, could move. Republic revived, groups of trees spat un....ily at onlookers, headed towards where energy was removed and produced. A lone woman, her husband an entomophiliac, his balls grossly shrunken from deviant acts, built kiosks stocked full of dynamite. Her deeds were ineffable, and the entire village, man, woman and child who had previously dwelled peaceably called for a diaspora with immediate effect and all agreed that a scout would go by the woman's shop, her livelihood burned, and deference won or they'd spin the wretched wench by her hair till her dreams spew into the desert for mirages and tanks to dispose of; boys volunteered but a tanned, freckly girl bounded forward with pineapple juice spilling from her shoes, soaking the council's clothes; overwrought with immeasurable gratitude, the elders fished deep from their souls and collectively gave the girl radiation tanks for safety, rendering her translucent; so seeking courage and some shelter, the little girl, certain victory, called loudly to the spirit world: 'lemons I send down, up to you these hundreds of fruits!' Spectres desired fruit, and so vengeance was granted, with two conditions: into their perdition she would go and free their souls and minds with virgin goats' urine; they'd piss along the yellow river called Frank, a victim of sociopathy, while she waits; when a plethora of fish commit brutal murder of the first degree, limits have been breached in that moment, and for the sake of memorabilia copper coloured pencils purporting to sell gems and apples would sing an operetta of fecundity onto twelve she-wolves. Second, up tunnels and wells alike she must ride. A beating heart, and a memory, powerful but small, she must find.

Peony Sauce

1

He stood over the misshapen grave, head bent in what he thought stood for respect. He didn't know what to do now that he was here, standing in front of it. He hadn't brought flowers with him. But there were wild flowers growing all around the graveyard – tall, deep orangey-red ones that looked like they were on fire. That seemed sufficient to Leon. Having looked on for a few minutes, he decided enough had been done and it was time to leave. Winding his way through the maze of graves, which were so old in places that they were sinking into the earth and lopsided, he felt sort of dizzy and almost upside-down. He stumbled more than once, and tried his best not to fall into the shallow pits down there. He had no desire to remain amongst the dead and was about ready to get home to his warm little flat.

When he finally reached what passed for a path in this place, his feet firmly on flat ground again, he started to march down it. On his right the glowing graveyard, and on his left the iron fence, keeping out passers-by on the street with its sturdy poles and fierce spikes. The road there was quiet, with no cars and no pedestrians messing up Leon's assumed stance of a solitary mourner. Along he went, bound for the gate. But as he approached one particularly grand tree, a glint caught his eye, and the glint kept glinting as he walked along, so that his gaze was directed entirely at this one spot where the glinting was happening. When he got there, Leon was amazed to discover a thing hanging from the branch of the offending tree. On closer inspection it turned out to be a piece of broken mirror hanging by a string. On even closer inspection he realised that the piece of mirror was not some kind of freak of nature but something placed there by a mystery person, because on the glass was scratched a little poem, or adage, or phrase, and it said:

poetry must be made by all

that's it, no more. He held it aloft between his fingers and pondered on it until the sentence was firmly locked into his long term memory and, bemused, he left the graveyard and caught the bus home.

When he got into his flat the heating was on too high and it was nastily warm, so he headed straight over to the thermostat to put the bastard in its place. He yanked the dial down to teach it a lesson and an hour or two later he was cold enough to shiver. To counter the cold, he ran a bath. Covered in suds, he traced the foam with his fingers and thought to himself, 'poetry must be made by all', and then he thought, 'why am I still thinking about that?' As he shampooed his hair he thought, 'poetry must be made by all', and then, 'what does it mean?' He lit a cigarette as he watched a late night porno and he thought 'poetry must be made by all', and then, 'I must find out what that means'.

That night he slept like a baby. In his dream he was back in the graveyard, except it wasn't a graveyard, it was the rooftop of some unknown building, and it was labyrinthine, and he was lost. He wandered around like a turkey without a brain until he found a little old woman and what else could she possibly have said to him but, 'poetry must be made by all', and he said to her, 'but what does it mean?' and she laughed at him, poor lost soul that he was. Enraged, he awoke with the sun that morning and the same phrase battered his brain, hammering down like hail upon it, until there was nothing to do but go back to the graveyard.

When he got there he quickly circumnavigated all the decrepit old stones and headed straight for his tree. His broken piece of mirror was still there and he yanked it off the string upon which it hung, stuffed it roughly into his bag, and headed out. What does it mean, what does it mean? That night he propped the mirror piece up on the wall behind his desk and stared at himself in it. He couldn't have told you how long he was there, and sometimes he saw his face, and sometimes the words, but always he heard them repeat in his mind until any meaning that was once applicable to them became totally obscured and all he could think was, 'poetry must be made by all, poetry must be made by all'.

The next day, a Monday, Leon had to go back to work. He asked all of his colleagues if they'd ever heard such a phrase, but none of them had, and no one seemed to care that he'd found it in a graveyard on a hanging broken mirror. When no one was watching him he called his mum and asked her, and got her to ask his father and then his brother, but they had no insight to provide either. After a quick lunch he rang around his closest friends, and then some not so close, and then people with whom he barely shared a relationship at all, and then any ex-girlfriends with whom he was still on speaking terms, but no light could be shed by any of them on the mystery phrase.

That night, back at the block of flats in which he dwelt he trudged up the stairs, passing a nameless neighbour who was on his way down. Leon grunted some sort of recognition noise, and then, in his desperation, asked this virtual stranger if his phrase meant anything to him.

The man, one foot on the landing of the fifth floor, one on the step going down, stopped in his tracks, looked up at Leon, and smiled.

"Poetry must be made by all," he repeated. "Poetry must be made by all...I haven't heard that in a while."

"But you *have* heard of it?" Leon asked anxiously.

"Yes, I've heard it said, many a time." The man hesitated, glanced at the stairs below him, and said, "Do you fancy a drink, mate?"

Together they headed into the man's flat. He handed Leon a cold beer and they sat opposite each other on his two sofas.

"Never really spoken to you, have I?"

Leon shook his head in agreement.

"Been living here a couple of years now. I'm Jacob."

"Leon," Leon said. "Six months."

"That all?"

Leon nodded.

"Well, then, about that thing. 'Poetry must be made by all'. God, that takes me back."

"Where to?"

"Childhood. Adolescence, actually. It was my gran. She used to say it. Constantly. Seriously, all the time. She was batty. I was twenty before I realised all old people aren't batty. 'Poetry must be made by all...and not by one.'"

Leon humoured the man with a smile and allowed a short time to pass in polite silence before pressing on: "So what does it mean?"

"I don't really know," Jacob replied, shaking his head ruefully. "Probably nothing. The woman was off her rocker."

Leon took a sip of his beer and thought for a moment. "But it must mean something. Why would two totally unconnected people know it otherwise? Unless your gran put that mirror in the graveyard?"

"What?"

"Oh – right." Leon related the genesis of his interest and waited for Jacob to respond. Jacob sat looking at Leon with a funny look on his face for a minute or two. Leon was just about to ask him what he meant by not saying anything, when Jacob piped up:

"Is this a joke?"

"A joke?"

"It's not funny, if it is. What are you playing at? Did you know my gran? Do you know something about her?"

"No, I – why? Look, I just found this mirror, I've had the phrase stuck in my head ever since, so I've been asking everyone I know about it. You're about the fiftieth person I've asked."

"My gran – when I say she was batty, I mean *she was batty*. I don't mean Alzheimers or dementia or anything, I mean from dawn till dusk and all night long she lived in her own world, barely recognising reality. She'd say all this completely arbitrary stuff and she wouldn't respond to anything you said to her. Sometimes she'd say something totally off the wall, and other times she'd say stuff that almost made sense, like she was trying to communicate really important things to us but didn't speak our language. That phrase – 'poetry must be made by all, and not by one' – is one that she said all the time."

"I see. Or, I don't, but, yes, I see."

"I don't understand it, but this must be a prank, though who would play it I can't think, and how they knew it'd get back to me…I mean, how did they know you'd see it, care about it enough to take it home, ask a neighbour you've barely spoken to before?"

"You've lost me completely."

"My gran. I mean, she's dead, right? So it can't be her. She didn't really have any friends as such, at least, not that I knew. But it's just too much to be a coincidence."

"Still lost."

Jacob sighed. "My gran. She's dead. Right? Dead and buried. And in your graveyard, where you found the mirror, is where she's buried. And then you find this mirror and ask me about it; me, a virtual stranger. It's weird. A bit *too* weird, if you get my meaning."

"I suppose it is," Leon concurred. The whole exchange had taken a turn he wasn't sure he understood. "Do you want to tell me about your gran some more?"

"Alright," Jacob said, taking a large swig of his beer. "But I'm going to need a fag. Now, I haven't smoked in two years, so I haven't got any tobacco. I don't suppose you have one you can offer me?"

"As a matter of fact, I do." Leon pulled out his packet of twenty and handed it and a lighter over to Jacob. Jacob lit up, coughed up, almost blacked out, and then sighed happily.

"First one's always a bit rough, and then it's like being admitted back into heaven."

"Tried to quit before, then?"

"Only eight or nine times. Oh, this is so good."

Leon waited patiently for Jacob to finish enjoying his cigarette. Meanwhile, he thought he might as well have one himself, and did so.

"Well, she was my maternal grandmother. About sixty when I was born, in her mid-seventies when she came to live with us. Yeah, she lived with us. I mean, she was off with the fairies, but somehow she was generally able to live alright if you bought her food and clothes and stuff. My mum'd go round there all the time to make sure she was eating and cleaning and getting out of bed. My mum said she wasn't so bad when she was a little girl. But she grew up with it, and what you grow up with you think is normal, right? So she hardly noticed that my gran was a bit loony. Her dad, my granddad, was dead by the time she was eight or so, so she had no frame of reference or anything.

"Anyway, I was a teen when she came to stay with us. We had a pretty reasonable sized house so she had a nice room on the opposite side of the house to me and I stayed out of her way, 'case she cornered me to say something weird. I was all hormonal and stuff, you know, I didn't want to deal with my mental gran. I'd see her shuffling down the stairs and wait until she was in the kitchen to come out of my room. When she talked to me I – and, look, I'm not proud of it – mostly I'd just ignore her. I mean, to me she was just, you know, talking to a giant purple squirrel or something, telling it to ride a pony into tomorrow. I don't know. Sometimes she'd touch my face, it made my skin crawl, I was a kid and my face had all this acne on it and she'd touch my cheek, *caress* it, oh, I hated it.

"I think I was about sixteen when they took her to the home. I was seriously relieved. Finally I could bring friends round without sneaking them upstairs, without worrying what she'd say to them. I did the odd requisite Christmas and birthday visit, nodded at her when she said her barmy things to me, and just ignored her existence other than that. No guilt, no remorse, nothing. Then one year, on my eighteenth birthday, she sent me a picture. It was a beautiful thing, a wolf with these glinting, hungry, eyes, it was amazing. On the back she hadn't written anything but 'poetry must be made by all'. It was the last thing she ever said to me: a week later she died."

Leon said nothing for a moment, waiting for the story to seep properly into his brain.

"Well," he said finally, "I can see why the mirror thing got to you, then."

"Yeah," Jacob said with a laugh. "So if you were put up to this by my brother or something, you really ought to tell me."

"Scout's honour, I just found this mirror."

"Scout's honour?"

"Yeah, well…you know. I'm not a religious man."

Jacob raised his eyebrows. "I haven't visited her grave in years. You want to go?"

Leon shrugged and put down his beer can. "Why not?"

"Now?"

"Why not?"

They each stood over the grassy mound. The headstone was all slanted and falling into the underworld to join with the soul of the occupant of the grave.

"There she is," Jacob said unnecessarily. "Should we do something?"

"Like what?"

"Well, you know," he said, gesturing to the mound. "Flowers? Prayer? A dance?"

"A dance?"

Jacob shrugged. "I dunno."

"Well we didn't bring any flowers and I don't pray. So dance it is." Raising his eyebrows in challenge, Leon began to sway. A little light in the furthermost corner of his brain flicked on saying 'you're drunk'. Leon flicked it off and carried on moving his hips. "Well?" he said to Jacob, moving clumsily, "What are you waiting for?" As if possessed, Jacob threw any ounce of sense he had left and starting moving. Neither really knew what dancing was, so the two of them just sort of jiggled their bodies around, an arm flailing occasionally, in front of the grave.

When they ran out of breath and needed to partake of liquid refreshment, Leon flopped onto the floor, which was damp with dusk-dew, and pulled a small bottle of vodka out of his bag. Frowning in puzzlement, Jacob said:

"Where did that come from?"

Leon smiled and replied, "It's my emergency stash."

Jacob paused, deciding whether or not to continue his line of questioning. Eventually he said, "Is this an emergency then?"

"Well," said Leon, casting his eyes about him, "I'm thirsty from all that dancing, and we've no other drink, so I'd say so, yeah." He took a swig and grimaced as the nasty cheap vodka burned a path down to his stomach. "Do you want some, or what?"

"Go on, then."

The two of them sat in harmonic silence, passing the bottle to and fro. Slowly the sun began to fall in the west, casting a red shadow around them, enhancing the wildflowers' colour so that the whole graveyard looked like the heart of a dying fire. When the vodka was finished they stood up, wobbling, with little inkling of what to do next. It seemed to the two men – whether it was the alcohol fogging their rationality, or the odd circumstances of their meeting – that something now existed between them, that they had been thrown together by some bizarre external force of the world, and that the beer and vodka had cemented the bond irrevocably; but that now, with the graveyard soon to be submerged totally in darkness and the vodka all settled warmly in their stomachs, the way forward was fuzzy and unclear. Stumbling slightly they aided, or rather hindered, one another along the path that ran alongside the iron fence of the graveyard, toward the gate. It was Jacob who first saw the blob, a shape made indistinct by his vodka eyes and the almost-faded light, hanging from the very tree which sent forth Leon's mirror those few days ago. He drew Leon's attention to it, and together they powered their way over to the hanging thing, pulled it off the tree, and each held it in his palm until they were ready to speak.

"What is it, Jacob?" Jacob had the thing in his hand and was eyeing it curiously.

"A globe, I think." The thing was certainly globe-shaped, but by now it was too dark to make out the markings on it, to see if it was in fact a globe of the world. "Let's take it back to mine."

Leon agreed and they made their way home, steadier now that they had purpose.

2

For all the world as if they had never embarked on their excursion, Leon and Jacob were sitting once again opposite one another, each on one of Jacob's two sofas, with two beers on a low table between them. The only slight difference now was the globe that passed between them, tossed from one hand to the other, from one man to the other, the entire while. One of them would catch it, turn it around and scrutinise it, tap it to hear what sound it made, peer at the tiny writing to see if anything was amiss, and, finding nothing, toss it to the other to ape the process.

"What do you think, then?" asked Leon.

"I don't know… it's just a globe, isn't it?"

And so it was. A little map of the earth on a sphere; here was England, there the Americas, over there in their correct position, Asia; each continent and country marked, as far as Leon and Jacob could tell, flawlessly, nothing to mark out this globe as unusual in any way.

"What's the point of it, then?"

"God only knows," replied Jacob. "Maybe there is no point. It's probably a prank, isn't it?"

"Some prank."

The conversation had swayed little from this general subject in an hour. They were beginning to sober up and become irritated.

"Here." Jacob lobbed the globe at Leon a little more forcefully than was necessary, and with quite a terrible aim, so that it missed him entirely, landed on the floor behind Leon's sofa, and rolled toward the front door. At that moment, the front door burst open, and a woman strode through it, her foot crashing down on the fragile little globe and crushing it beneath her.

She winced, screwing up her eyeballs tightly and stood stock still.

"Please tell me that wasn't a mouse," she said, eyes still shut. When no one replied, she peaked an eye open and saw with astonishment that Jacob and some bloke she didn't know were staring at her like she was covered in shit. "What?" she asked. "What did I step on?" Their gazes moved down to where her foot was still on top of the smashed globe. Tentatively she moved her foot away and bent down to retrieve the broken whatever-it-was. She scooped up the shards into her hand and looked at it. From the rubble, gingerly she plucked a piece of paper that had been folded again and again until it was half the size of a postage stamp; it had apparently been contained in the hollow of the globe. "What's this?" she asked Jacob. He still did not speak, merely goggled at her as if she were inhuman. Making a face at him, she crossed the room to the side cabinet, set down the pieces of globe, and unfolded the paper. Her eyes narrowed and her face screwed up tighter the more she revealed, until the whole thing was unfurled in front of her.

"This is a joke, right?" she asked, her heart beating fast, and for the first time she looked at this strange man in her living room, and found herself a little afraid. "Right, Jacob? Jacob?"

"…" Jacob's mouth opened as if to reply, but no words escaped him. The woman looked back at the paper she was still holding in slightly shaking hands, back up at Jacob, and back down at the strange man, who was staring at her with an equally unfathomable stare. Both of them seemed to have been rendered mute, for some reason.

"Jacob – will you speak to me, please? Hello? It's me, Peony?"

When she still received no response, Peony marched over to where her boyfriend was sitting and shoved the piece of paper in his lap.

"Jacob – is this a joke, or not?" She glanced at Leon, who had followed her with his eyes all the way to her current position, which was hands on hips in front of a bewildered-looking Jacob.

Slowly, Jacob took up the paper in his hand, and held it in front of his face. Still unspeaking, he looked back at his girlfriend, then at Leon, a tiny little smile creeping surreptitiously over his face, and he handed Leon the paper. Leon leaned in to take it, and sat back to look at it.

In front of him was a picture of three people. A woman and two men, all of whom looked rather similar with dark hair, pale skin, and made up faces, were standing sidelong to the camera. The woman and one of the men faced each other and were embraced in a passionate kiss. The second man stood behind the woman, planting a kiss on her shoulder, his hands on her hips and his body pressed up against hers. All three of them were naked. Leon marvelled at the picture, then touched it gently with a finger, and then looked up, to see Peony and Jacob standing before him, kissing wildly. Without giving his actions a second thought, he tossed the picture aside and kissed the back of Peony's neck, and she moaned into Jacob's mouth.

The next morning when Peony awoke, it was a few moments before she registered that there was a man lump asleep behind her and a man lump asleep in front of her, and it was another few seconds before she remembered why. Smiling to herself, she crept out of the bed, sliding herself off the front of it rather than risk waking one of the sleeping figures either side of her. She splashed her face and brushed her teeth, and then went into her kitchen and put the pot on to boil, and then, realising how utterly starving she was, put bacon on to cook.

She walked back into the bedroom armed with coffee and bacon sandwiches, and, waking each man with a kiss to the forehead, handed them each a plate and a mug. Instinct took over Leon and Jacob and they ate and drank hungrily before they were even properly awake. When all three were finished, they exchanged guilty looks at each other, each remembering the previous night's debauchery from their own angle, each one amazed at their own misbehaviour and totally turned on by the memory of it. Peony risked a glance down at Leon's crotch, and felt an ache in her own when she realised he was completely hard. Gently he took her hand and placed it on his erection, and when she leant in to take him orally, she felt the weight shift behind her and Jacob move up behind her, and she let her mind roam free as she allowed herself once again to indulge total sybaritism.

Laying back with Jacob playing with her hair and Leon holding her hand, Peony finally found her voice.

"Jacob, I've got to ask you – how did you know?"

"Know what, my darling?"

"Well," she laughed. "You know. This."

Jacob sat up abruptly, forcing Peony to sit up too. "What do you mean?"

She frowned at him. "Well – the globe. And the picture?"

He shook his head. "What?"

"Well I mean, it was quite an elaborate way of going about it, don't you think? And asking Leon over before I'd even said yes, and somehow getting me to step on it as I came in-"

"Wait," Jacob said, interrupting her. "You think I arranged this?"

She eyed him suspiciously. "Are you saying you didn't?"

"Yes."

"I'm confused."

Jacob tried to explain the circumstances of his and Leon's acquaintance, recounting the graveyard times and the discovery of the globe and the sitting in the flat wondering what the hell it was and what to do with it until she stepped on it.

"You mean to say that it was a complete coincidence that I stepped on this globe, found the pornographic picture, it just so happened that a fantasy of mine was depicted on this picture, and it was pure luck that there were two ready and willing blokes in the room to make it so right there and then?"

"Basically, yes."

She turned to Leon. "Is this the truth?" Leon affirmed it. "I don't know what to make of all this. It's weird."

"Well," said Leon, "why don't we take you to the graveyard, so you can see it for yourself?"

"Al – alright," she said slowly, and they all dressed and made their way back down to the graveyard.

"I never much liked her, but if she's reaching from the beyond to save our relationship, I must say that she's gone up in my estimations."

"You didn't like my gran?"

"Well… you know…she was creepy."

Jacob sighed. "Yeah, she was."

"What now?" Peony was eager to get away from this particular headstone.

They both turned to Leon as if he were the natural leader of this peculiar outing.

He shrugged. "I guess we take a look at the tree, you know – see if there's anything new there."

Peony's eyes lit up, all a-glimmer. This, aside from the frenetic sex she'd engaged in last night, was the wildest thing she'd done in many a month; perhaps, she thought, many a year. She was desperate for there to be something on the tree: desperate, she was. With each of her arms linked into the two men's arms, Peony ambled with Jacob and Leon across the uneven ground towards their tree. This time, with all of their eyes fixated directly on the tree as they approached it – Leon having pointed out to Peony which one it was – they all saw from a great distance that there was indeed a third object hanging from their tree.

Peony pulled it down. She pulled the lid off the small black tube, and twisted the bottom so that the finger of lipstick protruded upwards like a tongue. She frowned at it, disappointed. What good was a lipstick to them? She handed it to Leon.

"Well," he said. "The other two things required some homework, some digging, right? I mean, the phrase on the mirror brought me to you-" he looked at Jacob "-and the globe meant nothing to Jacob and me, but brought us, or me, anyway, to you-" he smiled at Peony "-so maybe this has some other meaning that will take us somewhere else."

"That makes sense," Jacob agreed, nodding, "but where are we actually going with these? I mean, is it like a treasure hunt, or what? Where does it end? Do we just keep coming back to this tree and let it dictate our actions, or what?"

Nobody spoke for a while. Not really knowing what else to do to break the tension, Peony took back the lipstick and applied it to her lips. It was an action she'd performed countless times before so she was able to do it perfectly without the aid of her reflection. When she was finished,

Jacob and Leon were both looking at her in awe.

"What?"

"It looks like blood," they said in unison, looked at each other, then back at Peony.

"Oh. Well, here." She passed the stick to Leon.

"What do you want me to do with it?"

"Put it on, of course."

Leon, biting back his initial reaction to her demand, shrugged and obeyed. Unskilled, unlike Peony, he made a hack job of it. As the lipstick passed to Jacob for application, Peony used the tip of her finger to even up Leon's attempt, and then did the same for Jacob. They all stood looking at each other under their tree, their blood-red mouths making them resemble animals sated with carrion, except they were all startled, and confused.

"And now what?" This time it was Leon who asked the question.

"We go out." Leon turned to look at Peony.

"Out? Out where?"

"Drinking."

"Looking like this?"

"Not exactly, no. Let's go back to the flat."

When they got there, Peony touched up all of their lips with the lipstick, then applied eyeliner and black eye shadow to each man. They acquiesced without a word. When she was finished with that, she dressed them in the clothes she decided fit best with the make up, lending Leon some of Jacob's, and carefully chose her own outfit. She felt her logic abandoning her as she regressed to the state of a child, joyfully dressing up her dolls, who would be mute and thus unable to protest. When she was satisfied, she sat them in the living room and refused to give in to their requests for mirrors; it made little difference, though, as they could see each other, and so infer from the other's look what their own must be. But if either of them was horrified or reluctant, they hid it and meekly sat awaiting Peony's next instruction.

"Well then. Now we go out."

Jacob cleared his throat.

"What is it?" Peony asked.

"Well," he began. "It's eleven-thirty in the morning, we're dressed like girls and I was supposed to be at work three hours ago."

"What's your point?"

"..." Jacob opened his mouth to retort, but, finding none, closed it again.

"OK," Peony said, clearly considering the matter settled, "shall we have one for the road?" And out of nowhere she produced three measures of gin, handed them round, and toasted to their health before seeing hers off in one gulp. With one last look at his girlfriend, Jacob swallowed his down, and when he looked over at Leon, Leon's glass was already empty and there was a pink flush accompanying the early drinking that crept over his cheeks like blusher.

"Let's go."

3

The first place they reached was a converted church. It seemed fitting so they went in. All three of them were dragged to Sunday services as children and so, at first, felt the conditioned response to the high ceilings and ornate windows – reverent silence. But when they reached the bar, there was a long panelled mirror spanning the length of it, and one glance at their reflections was enough to shake them out of their trance. The men were not surprised at their own appearances, but shocked nonetheless: their makeup was heavy and their clothes, whilst not outlandish, were not the sort they wore to work on a weekday or lounged about in at the weekend; they were showy, proud clothes. Peony hardly recognised her own figure, marvelling at the shape she cut in the dress she'd chosen to wear – a vampish black thing that she'd bought for a fancy dress party and not even had the balls to wear then. But what stood out more than anything was the garish red staining on their lips, so powerful to look at that their other clothes were black and white in comparison.

They each furnished themselves with their choice of drink – neat whiskey for Leon, a gin-and-tonic for Jacob, and a large red wine (which she didn't usually drink, but felt a irrepressible urge for now) for Peony. In the soft décor of the bar the three of them stood out a mile, and the other punters were only drinking half-pints with their lunches; everyone stared at them, as they stood at the bar in comfortable silence, each thinking their own thoughts and sipping on their drinks.

When they were finished there they headed out to find another place and came upon a smoky wooden pub with guest ales, which they decided to sample. As there were six guest ales they each had two pints there, the barman giving the men filthy looks and slightly confused ones to Peony, before Leon caught a middle-aged man muttering "fucking poofs" under his breath to his bitter and felt it was probably time to leave. Next they came to a large pub that was part of a bigger chain, and they sat in a corner sharing a jug of Long Island Iced Teas, their noise attracting as much attention to them as their looks now. When he went to the toilet, Jacob smiled to himself when a rather dashing young man gave him a dazzling, unmistakably flirtatious grin. After that they decided it was time for food so they ducked into a noodle restaurant, munched up their chow meins and beers, and stole a load of chopsticks.

By the time they reached the fourth building day was turning into evening and pubs were filling up with people enjoying their post-work freedom. They stumbled into a crowded bar full of suits, ordered some shots and long drinks, and squeezed into a corner table, where Peony spent the entire time batting down the advances of horny rich men, leaving Leon and Jacob to converse with each other. At the other end of the bar they noticed another pair of men, dressed not so very differently from themselves, with their hands entwined. When they saw Leon and Jacob looking, they winked, a knowing, encouraging wink. Leon and Jacob looked away quickly, embarrassed at first, but then, slowly looking up at each other, they grinned.

Slowly, so very slowly, Leon leaned in to Jacob and brushed his lips with his own. Just touching like that for a while, neither man moved, just allowed themselves to get used to the sensation. Then, just as slowly, Leon moved out again, his eyes on Jacob the whole time. He raised his eyebrows as if for consent, and when Jacob smiled sedately, Leon launched himself on his new stranger-friend, and kissed him with sun-fire. While this was going on, Peony was enjoying her role as temptress, lapping up the attentions of several different men at once, and relishing in her assumed indifference to their flirtations. She hadn't even noticed that her boyfriend and Leon were wrestling tongues behind her, so that when, fed up of the tenacity of one man, she decided to put him off once and for all.

"I *am* here with my boyfriend, you know," she said to the man beside her, who was wearing a blue suit and the fashionable facial hair of the time.

"Oh, really?" asked the man contemptuously, glancing sidelong as her companions. "And which one is your boyfriend, exactly? The one with his tongue in the other one's mouth, or the one with his hand on the other one's thigh?"

Frowning at the man, she turned her head and saw the embracing pair. At her movement Jacob noticed Peony's attention turning to them and he broke away from Leon. He'd heard the conversation, being not two feet from the blue-suited man, and hadn't registered it until now. But without the slightest inkling of hesitation, he looked directly at the man and said,

"We both are."

Leon, quick to pick up on the situation, also turned his attention to Peony and confirmed, with his arm around Peony and his hand still on Jacob's thigh,

"That's right: we both are."

The suited man, knowing a lost cause when he saw one, shrugged to feign his indifference, and he and his companions turned away from Peony. Peony's eyes flashed as she looked from Jacob to Leon, Leon to Jacob.

"Well. Isn't this a turn up for the books. Did either of you know you were queer?"

"We're not," they said in unison.

"Mm hm," she said, voicing her disbelief. "Anyway, this place is getting boring. Shall we hit a club?"

They found themselves in a first-floor club, the type where people queue outside the doors for an hour waiting to hand over their score just to get past the bouncers. Peony, Jacob and Leon breezed past the crowd, hand in hand, exuding so much confidence that the door staff made no attempt to turn them away, merely stepping past to admit them. Upstairs, sitting in leather chairs around a low table, Peony knocked an entire bottle of red wine over with her foot, its contents glugging out over the waxed floor while the three of them looked like a big mass of limbs belonging to one wide monster. They got up and moved to the centre of the room, and danced like savage beasts, the lipstick that once adorned their mouths now so smeared across their faces that they looked wild and bloody, on a dance floor where there was always room for them wherever they roamed. When they managed to find their way back to the seats, all breath spent and in need of refreshment, they picked up drinks that weren't theirs and knocked them back.

On a stage behind the dance floor a band embarked on a long rhythmic song and the three lovers meandered back over to watch. Enthralled by the music, which somehow seemed familiar as if they knew it from a dream, they gazed up at the singer in raptures. Oblivious to their attentions the man muttered out the words to his song, his eyes shut in concentration, or delight.

"Did anybody see this snowman, standing in the wind alone?"

Peony, Jacob and Leon swayed instinctively to the beat.

A moment later a large man dressed in black tapped Leon on the shoulder, a storm over his face, and suddenly they were gone, running down the street, laughing so much they forgot how to speak.

Though no one was leading the way they managed somehow to end up back at Jacob and Peony's little flat. The cold penetrated them not at all, and, still laughing, the bedroom door was flung open and all three of them burst in at the same time. Peony, catching sight of her reflection, stumbled over to her mirror to investigate her face. She espied in the corner of her eye Leon and Jacob laying down next to one another, and she pretended to be really interested in cleaning up her make-up to give them time to explore each other.

She saw them kissing passionately, shyly exploring each other's familiar but unknown male anatomy; Leon stroking Jacob's stubbled cheeks and gripping his short hair, Jacob feeling Leon's chest and back, familiarly hard, but unfamiliarly beautiful. Tentatively they moved downwards, one man exploring the other's buttocks, the other brushing past his crotch. Peony felt it was time to join them, and approached them, silent as the grave. Still joint at the mouth Jacob and Leon glanced up at Peony and motioned for her to join in. They parted to make space for her, and she slipped in between their bodies, facing Leon. As she kissed him, the first man she'd kissed besides Jacob in years, his exciting, unfamiliar technique was accompanied by the warm, familiar caresses of Jacob behind her. The night of passion the three of them had shared the previous night seemed a million miles away and almost juvenile, because Peony had been reluctant to engage in affectionate intimacy with Leon, and Jacob had been too guarded of Peony to allow it. But now she was giving Leon her all, kissing him with love, and he her. The men quickly rid themselves of their clothes, and found themselves in the same position as they were last night: Leon lying before Peony, Jacob behind. Leon pulled up Peony's slip of a dress around her hips and entered her with ease, pulling a groan from her scarlet lips. Behind her, she felt Jacob do the same, but more slowly, more gently. As they found a steady, comfortable rhythm, Peony wet her fingers in her mouth, reached around Leon's backside, and carefully, slowly enough to give him time to protest, entered him with a finger. He gasped into her mouth, but allowed her to continue, and she moved in and out of him, increasing the pressure, and, when she thought he was ready, added another finger. This time he moaned, slightly in pain, slightly in pleasure, and she continued her ministrations as his thrusts became harder and more forceful. Jacob, seeing the spectacle, became even more aroused and increased his own speed and pressure. As the two men panted and gasped, Peony mustered the will-power to stop the men, push them both away, and slip off the bed. She stood at the end of it, and looked at the two men, who were staring at her as though she'd just cancelled Christmas.

"Come here, both of you," she said. They each rolled off the bed and stood up; as they walked around it to join Peony at the foot, she sat down. "Here, Leon," she said, and drew him down to her; leaning back, she guided him back into her. The bed was raised high enough off the ground that he did not need to kneel to do so; and then Jacob, realising what Peony had planned, grabbed their lube from the drawer, and sidled up against Leon's rear. Leon stiffened slightly, but allowed Jacob to caress him. Leon leant in to Peony to kiss her, giving Jacob better access, and then, without Peony's gentleness, Jacob pushed himself into Leon. Leon cried out at the intrusion and Jacob waited, buried inside Leon, until Leon relaxed. Very slowly, Jacob began to build up a pace, and when he was comfortable Leon continued to thrust into Peony, until he able to take more speed and depth from Jacob, and then more, and then Jacob's thrusts into Leon causes Leon to take Peony deeper, as she laid back on the bed. With Peony screaming her delight, both men came quickly. Leon was delirious in his pleasure but yet aware of his pain, though he found he didn't mind it too much. All spent and overcome with drunkenness and satiation, they crawled into bed and fell into deep slumbers.

The morning brought them hangovers but no regrets. After breakfasts and showers they didn't know what else to do but fuck again. When that was over they supposed they had better go back to the graveyard and see what was what.

They didn't bother to go and see they graves; neither the first one Leon was originally visiting, nor Jacob's grandmother's grave. They headed straight for their tree instead. None of them knew whether or not they were expecting to see something there; if they'd really have thought about it they probably would have realised that they had come to some sort of hiatus, or even an ending. So no one was really shocked, though they all registered disappointment, when they found nothing at their tree.

"I want to give the tree something back," Leon said.

"What for?" asked Jacob.

"I dunno, just feel like I should give it something, it's given me quite a lot."

The three stood in silence, wondering what gift would be fitting for the tree. Finally Peony shrugged herself out of her jacket and hung it on a branch.

"There," she said. Jacob and Leon nodded their approval. Peony shivering a little, the three of them headed down the rickety path to the gate and left the graveyard forever.

For Merl, who made the mirror.

Stuff on my floor

This mask lying on the floor
Doesn't make me want you more
A chilblain on my little toe
Doesn't count as sucker blow
What's new is fierce and that's what counts
A bitty lit, a bouncy wounce
A frugal nun, and not much more,
Is lying dead upon my floor.

Autobeauty

When I get around by automobile a rush of blood goes to my feet when I hit accelerate, closely preceded by blood to the head and followed by blood to the groin. In one simple movement I feel the surge of emotion from thrill to action to arousal, it's a beautiful thing. One time I hit something over a tonne and nearly caused carnage on the M11. Then the blood went all to my heart and I saw my own death, it was a beautiful thing. Now I sometimes kill pigeons for the same rush, that glimpse of horror before a thing dies. You'll never have seen such beauty, I'll warrant.

Being a boy, or a man, or something

Little man, little boy, cry if you please
Eighty-eight freight trains will not carry thee
So whine if thou will, thou contemptible oily cunt
And I shall be your running-mate, isn't that what you want?
Or throw up your hands and beg for a body,
Beg for your dinner, beg for a doggy,
All shall be yours if you wish it, just say the word, and I shall do it,
But I require a favour, in return, it's fair, and you like rules:
Just cut up all your clothes and set them on fire, and I shall give you
jewels.
Bejewelled man, bejewelled boy, why do you cry?
Is it because I'm only little and cannot reach the sky?
Give me a boot up, give me a boot, make me tall and make me coy, let me
fight and let me toy, and I'll be a man, my son, and I'll be a boy.

Crunch

Never let it be said that I fail when it comes to opening the pockets of miserly old bastards. I'm not good at much! But damn it all, I'm good at that. On the eleventh night of November, I was at home, eating chicken, when a small tap-a-tap-tapping arrived at my door, and who should be there, but my favourite miserly old bastard of the time, one Henry J. Rambold of the Rotterby fame. He wasn't smiling, as I never would have expected him to be. I wasn't in a terrible mood, though, so I invited him in for some paté. A small plate, just enough to piss him off, with the requisite three crackers and a glass of milk with a little dash of lime to make it taste totally shit. He ate the lot, devilishly greedy bastard miser as he was, and sat upon my faux-fur armchair that I so cherished, as well he knew. We made no conversation attempts as I waited for him to finish my victuals and get to the point as quickly as possible.

"Poison," he said. He didn't mutter it, he said it. "Poisoned fish, of all things."

"But you didn't eat it?"

"Not at first, of course. You could smell it a mile away. But you know, Vicky, these are hard times for the lot of us. It's not like I can pass these things up without weighing all possibilities together, in a list."

"Of course," I granted, inclining my head.

"Anyway, I was surveying the situation in my way, you know, un-affected by the marketing, by the glitz and glamour. But I was distracted all the while by the damn cat pawing at my lap. Give me the fish! I heard it thinking. I want it! It's mine! Well I couldn't have that, so I ate it. And what of it?" His shoulders hunched as he uttered the last words. A challenge, so I thought.

"Fight me, then. Fight me, and have done with it. I won't stand for this tomfoolery in my own house."

"Don't be a fool," he said, shrinking, "You know I don't fight haemophiliacs. Not after last time."

"Then shut the hell up and drink this." I handed him a goblet of steaming wine, which he reluctantly took and knocked back.

"Thanks. I guess I'll be going now," what with the score settled, I finished internally.

"Not so fast, old man. I haven't been paid."

"Think I'm paying you, you've a mind full of shite," he said, getting up.

I sighed. "What'll it take?"

He hesitated. "A week's laundry, a blow job from your lad, and an evening with the cat."

"Three days and a hand job."

He grunted. "Fine." He stood to leave. We shook hands like business partners ought, and he bowed out.

Anna the Clone

Jessica blinked at what she assumed must be an apparition, or a mirror, or her own insanity, staring back at her. Then she blinked again. Then she passed out.

"Come on – come on – come on –" something was saying, like a stuck record.

"Fuck *off*," Jessica mumbled. "Fuck *off* – fuck *off* – fuck *off* –"

"Come *on* – come *on* – come *on* –"

Cuck*oo* – cuck*oo* – cuck*oo*, she thought. OK, it's alright, I've just lost my mind. I must have experienced a trauma or something, and now I'm insane. And though I *think* I am hearing the sound of my own clone telling me to come on, and though I *think* I'm telling it over and over to fuck off, in fact I'm almost certainly just lying on a bed in an institution, my limbs tied to the bed posts, my mouth oozing dribble as my body absorbs the tranquilisers they're injecting into my blood.

She flicked an eye open. Her clone smiled in relief.

"Thank God!" it said. "I thought you were going to die of shock. The irony might have killed me too, and that'd make for the most unusual suicide of all time, don't you think?"

"Didn't I tell you to fuck off? Maybe I was being too ambiguous. Fuck off and *die!*"

"You don't mean that, Jessica; you don't mean it because I'm essentially your child, and I know us, we're not capable of infanticide."

"What do you mean, *I know us*? I'm not you and you're not me, I'm me and you're…a hallucination."

"Yeah, I knew you'd say that."

"Shut up, fuck off, and *die!*"

The thing that looked exactly like Jessica but wasn't her sighed loudly. "You're not being very nice, you know. I'm newborn. You should show me the ropes and things."

"Come off it. If you're my clone, you know exactly what I know."

"Not really. I think exactly like you think, and I have your knowledge and memories; but I don't *really* have the experiences."

"If you're newborn, how come you can talk?"

"I don't even know why I exist, how am I supposed to know why I can talk? "

"None of us know why we exist, you know, it's not just you."

"Really?"

"Yes, really. Oh God, why am I talking to my own hallucination?"

"Because you know deep down that you're not imagining me."

"*Yes I am.*"

"Fine Jessica, be a bitch. But I'm the same as you, remember, and I can be a bitch too. Why don't I just go and find my own way around? I think I'll go and find Bob first..."

"Don't you touch Bob!"

"Where is Bob now, I wonder? At work, I suppose?"

"I'll kill you if you go near him!"

"And commit suicide? I know we're not capable of that, Jessica."

"It's not suicide, it's murder, and you might not be, but I am, and if you go anywhere near my husband I'll slice open your throat with a butter knife and watch you bleed to death over the course of five hours, and while you die in the most agonising way I'll feel nothing but smugness because I'll know I've killed my insanity."

"Whatever you say, Jessica. I'm out of here. You could have been nicer to me."

The clone turned and walked out of Jessica's peripheries, and then her peripheries turned black, as she passed out again.

When she awoke, Jessica was blind. Actually, it was just night and the lights were off, but at first she thought she was blind. Then she realised she was in bed, which was definitely not where she'd passed out earlier. She sat up abruptly in a panic and thought she heard her own stomach-churning tinkle of a laugh, which meant her hallucination was still around somewhere. And then she heard her own laugh being followed by a deeper one, which she recognised as Bob's.

"Bitch, I'm going to kill you!" she shouted. Seconds later footsteps thudded towards her room and her door was yanked open. Bob's silhouette blocked the light streaming in through to the bedroom from the hallway.

"You're up!" he cried redundantly. "Come and see who's here, Jessica, you're not going to believe it!"

"If it's a usurping motherfucker who looks exactly like me, you better get her out of here because I'm going to decapitate her."

"That's right, it's your twin sister Anna!"

"Bob, you stupid simpleton, I haven't got a twin sister, she's a usurping hallucination and I've got to kill her. Shit, if you can see her you must be part of this elaborate dream sequence too; damn, I'm going to have to kill you too."

"Come and see her, then, Jessica, she's come a bloody long way to see you, you know. We've been having a spot of tea in the kitchen; she's been telling me all about you."

"How can she know anything about me, she didn't exist yesterday!"

Bob sat on the bed and felt Jessica's temperature. "I think you're delirious, honey. Are you feeling OK?"

"Of course I'm delirious, that's what I've been trying to tell you, moron!"

"Right, I'm calling 999, you're really ill, Jessica." Bob pushed Jessica back into a lying-down position. She sat up and screamed:

"Piss off!" and then she head-butted him. Bob looked in utter disbelief at his wife as, his nose pouring with blood, he keeled over and fainted. Jessica looked up to see her clone standing at the doorway. She was smiling.

"Told you I'd find Bob. He's really nice. I can't believe you just nutted him. You're a bit of a psycho. How can *you* be psycho and I be perfectly normal if I'm your clone?"

"How come you can tell him about me, huh? If you haven't got my memories, huh?"

"I've *got* your memories, I told you. And besides, I've got your capacity to lie."

"I don't lie!"

"But you've got the capacity built into your genetic make-up."

"How do you know about genetic make-up? *I* don't know about genetic make-up."

"I don't. Bob told me."

"Good, well, I'm glad we've got that sorted, because now I can kill you."

"You can't kill me now. Bob knows about me now, he'll notice my absence."

"I'm going to kill him too."

"Your own husband?"

"My own insanity!"

"We're not hallucinations!"

"Yes you are!"

Anna the clone looked at Jessica, as though she were trying to figure out a way to reason with her. Then she bolted out of the room. Before Jessica had a chance to react, she'd heard the front door bang shut and the clone was long gone. Once again, Jessica's mind went blank and she passed out.

Bob groaned as his eyes slowly opened. Immediately shooting pains darted across his nose and eyes and he raised a hand to touch his face. He felt dried, congealed blood stuck to it and the memory of being taken down by his ill, delirious wife flooded back into the forefront of his brain, and he groaned again. He sat up and took stock of the room. Jessica was breathing evenly, her body lain across the bed at a bizarre angle. He shifted her into a proper lying position, then sat down in front of the mirror on her bedside desk to assess the damage. He couldn't see properly; it was still night, the bedroom light was off, and the only light came in softly through the open door from the hallway. Bob reached over to switch the lamp on. He sat back, looked in the mirror, and screamed.

A figure stood in the corner of the room, watching Bob's movements.

"Who the fucking hell are you?" Bob screamed.

"I don't really know, Bob, but I know who you are and I know that I came from you."

"Why have you got my *face*?"

"I told you; because I came from you."

"Came from me, came from me, came from me?!"

"Yep."

"What does *that mean*? Oh – oh, shit, oh for fuck's sake, I get it," he said, calming down. "I've caught whatever Jessica's got. Oh, thank God, I'm just hallucinating. Yes, that makes sense; Jessica thought her sister Anna was an hallucination, so now I'm ill I'm imagining the same. Thank the Lord."

"Yeah, that's wrong. I'm a real thing, I'm your own being but not you, a physical extension of you, like a baby, only not."

"Yes, Thing, you're as real as Father Christmas. Go away now, I'm going to go to bed and have a nap and when I wake up I expect you to be gone."

"Don't call me Thing," the thing said angrily. "I'm no better or worse than you."

"Of course you are. Away now, I sleep now."

"Where am I to go? I need you, Bob!"

"Yes, I know, you need me to exist, which is why I'm going to get myself better so you'll fuck off."

"That's just cold."

"What can I say, we're a cold couple of bastards, alright?"

By this time Bob had crawled into bed next to his wife and pulled the covers up to his chin.

"Night night, Thing," he said. "Don't forget to turn the hall light off on your way out." And he fell asleep.

The Thing, the Bob-clone, looked sadly down at his creator. He turned and left the room. As he crept out of the front door, he turned off the hallway light.

He roamed the streets, not understanding where he was or what he ought to do. After several hours of roaming he began to feel the first pangs of hunger. He knew he needed money to buy food but didn't have any; he knew he needed to have a bank account to store his money and a job to earn it, but he had neither or those; and so, in desperate need of the first meal of his existence, he snatched a burger off a passing woman, who looked angry but hurried away. After his burger he felt thirst; unable to find a free source of clean water, he settled for drinking the foul-tasting water of a pond in a park. Finally he felt fatigue, and he laid down under a tree and fell asleep.

Anna the Clone too roamed the streets for several hours. But Anna had Jessica's genes and in them the sort of instinctive sharpness and immorality that Bob's clone lacked; and she lacked the deep sense of pride that Bob had. So she had the sense to nick Jessica's bag as she ran out, and with it money, and the house keys. She spent an hour in a café, eating a tasty meal and drinking nice clean water. Then she weaved in and out of the shops, reading product labels with interest, knowing somehow what they were, though she was seeing them for the first time of her life. As she handled a handbag she knew Jessica would love, she arrived at an idea. And because she had the mental map drawn a few weeks ago by Jessica when she and Bob had a little accident, she knew exactly where to go to execute it.

"Hello," the bored-looking receptionist greeted her. "Can I help you?"

"I'd like to see a doctor."

"Name?" Anna gave her all the requisite details. "Have a seat."

After a dull half an hour, Anna was called in to see the doctor.

"Hello, Jessica," the doctor said. "What can we do for you today?"

"I need some better sleeping pills."

"You didn't have any luck with the ones I prescribed you?"

"I keep waking up in the middle of the night." This much, at least, was true. Or would be, if Anna and Jessica were interchangeable.

"Alright. I'll try you on something stronger. Do you want dissolvable ones again?"

"Yes, please," Anna said, smiling.

"OK. Dissolve one tablet in water and drink before bed. That should last you all night. Don't take more than one, though; if you're still not sleeping through, come and see me again."

"Yes, Doctor. Thank you." Anna collected the pills from the pharmacy; popped into a herbal remedies shopped and picked up some smelling salts; and headed to what she was utterly convinced was 'home'.

When she got back to the house, she dissolved all but one of the sleeping tablets into one glass of water, and left it on the table. She crept back upstairs and, as quietly as she could manage, without waking Bob, she slid Jessica off the bed and pushed her under it. Then she got into bed and prodded Bob awake.

"Bob," she said in a croaky voice. "Bob, I can't sleep. I went downstairs and made myself a sleeping draught but I was too weak to carry it up. Will you get it for me?"

"Oh, alright, honey," he said meekly, convinced that he too was sick. As soon as Bob was out of the door, Anna the Clone got Jessica back out from under the bed and shoved her onto it. She waved the smelling salts in front of her and as she slowly came round, Anna the Clone got under the bed. Bob re-entered the room, carrying the draught.

"Here you go," he said, holding the glass out to Jessica. She moaned and said nothing. Sighing, he deigned to hold it to her lips and help her drink. Obediently she sipped it down, a little at a time, until most of it was gone. "I'm sure that'll do it," he whispered, as she nodded off. Anna the Clone held her breath and waited for Bob to fall back to sleep. When he was snoring again, Anna the Clone crept into the hallway, yanked the thermostat up, switched places with Jessica again and waited with baited breath for Bob to wake up.

It had been morning for several hours before he did awake. He was sweating profusely. Anna the Clone was also hot but had cooled herself off in the bathroom periodically throughout the night. As soon as he awoke Anna pounced on him.

"You've got a temperature," she said. "Go back to sleep."

"Are you better now?" he croaked.

"All better. Here, I've already been to the chemist's; he said you should take this." She held out a glass of water into which she'd mixed the remaining sleeping tablet. "It'll lower your temperature and help you sleep better."

Bob allowed himself to be fed the mixture. It wasn't long before he was back in the land of nod. Anna the Clone dragged Jessica's body down the stairs and looked at it for a while. She wasn't sure what to do with it. After a lot of deliberation, she covered it with a blanket and dragged it into the garage. There she hacked it to bits with an axe and put all the bits in a bag. Then, leaving the bag in the garage, she drove Jessica's car to the garden centre and learnt how to drain a garden pond and fill it up again. Into the empty pond the body-bag went, and on top of it, the cement. Her work had taken all day but Bob was still asleep when she went to check on him. She took a load of washing out of the basket and put it on to wash in the machine.

It was his third day of sleeping rough, and Bob's clone had been stealing to eat and sleeping in the park. He soon discovered that the benches were taken by other homeless men and fiercely guarded, so he slept on the hard dirt beneath his tree. He thought constantly about Bob, and Bob's duty to care for his clone, which he had cruelly forsaken. But Bob's clone's pride was such that he couldn't bear to return to his maker, after such an unceremonious dumping.

He was cold. He was hungry. He was despondent, depressed, and rejected, hugging the blanket that he'd bought from a charity shop with the couple of quid he'd mugged someone for. One of the long-term homeless men of the park, who went by the name of Jim, sidled over to him and said, "I'll have that, my lad."

"What now? I haven't got anything!"

"That blanket. It's mine, you stole it, give it back. We don't like thieves round here."

"It's mine!"

Jim yanked Bob's clone to his feet, snatched the blanket away, and punched him in the stomach.

"Steal my stuff again and you'll get worse."

Jim walked off, leaving Bob's clone to sink back down to the floor and hug himself with his arms, a poor substitute for the blanket. He began to cry, as quietly as he could manage.

As darkness fell around him and coldness enveloped and numbed him, Bob's clone began to wonder if he should just jump into the river. There was only room for one Bob in this world, and no one cared about the other one. No one wanted him.

A figure loomed over Bob's clone. Fearing Jim again, Bob cowered back into his tree.

"Fancy a meal?" the figure said.

"What?"

"You hungry?"

"Yes - I'm starving."

"Come on then; let me buy you a burger."

Hardly believing his luck, he followed the stranger to a McDonald's, where he enjoyed an enormous meal and a coke.

"You got anywhere to stay?" the strange man asked. Bob's clone shook his head. "Come on then; you can stay at mine, if you like."

Bob's clone was a newborn, but he was not born yesterday. He knew the score. Sort of. Yet here was the first person in Bob's clone's meagre existence to want him; and not even to hit him, steal from him, or spit on him. Bob's clone nodded meek acquiescence and they headed to a flat nearby.

The man let Bob's clone use the shower - the first wash of his existence. That night Bob's clone earned himself a night on the couch and a tenner, and he left in the morning feeling defiant, knowing that he would be going back that night, and that he would have somewhere warm to stay and another tenner tonight. After that night he stayed with one of the strange man's friends, and then a friend of his, until he'd become friendly with half a dozen more men.

Soon Bob's clone got a bit of a name for himself; and from that, he got an actual name. They called him Johnny; and with his name came a degree of unwelcome fame. When the area's pimp got to know about him, he sent round a bunch of his minions to tell Johnny that he was working for him now. He gave Johnny a dirty room to stay in and some food. The next day Johnny saw eight blokes, none of them his friends, and no money. The day after that he only saw six men, but the last one beat him so badly he couldn't see another for a week.

One day, when Johnny had been beaten again and so had the morning off, he went and sat by the river, wondering again if he mightn't just chuck himself in it. Suddenly, he looked over to the river edge and saw a lady, in a red coat, walking a pointless little dog. He recognised her, yet didn't recognise her. Then he gasped, understanding who she was. He tried to make his mind work, think of what he wanted to say to her, but nothing came, and then, she was gone, getting in her car and driving away from him. That afternoon, he throttled his final client, robbed him, and ran, feeling his way back to Bob's house. He rang the doorbell.

Anna the Clone answered. She narrowed her eyes and covered her nose to close the smell off to her nasal passage.

"What is it?"

"Hello, Anna."

"I'm Jessica."

"I want to see Bob, Anna."

Anna the Clone's eyes widened. "I told you, I'm Jessica. You're not Bob's brother, by any chance, are you?"

"Sort of."

"His clone?"

"Funny how you knew that, isn't it, *Jessica*?"

"Get in here." She yanked him inside so roughly that he fell to the floor. "You're not welcome. What do you want?"

"I want help! Look at what's happened to me!"

"Bob doesn't care and neither do I. Bugger off."

"Please!" Bob's clone said, supplicating Anna the Clone on his knees. "Please, Anna!"

"Stop calling me that! I'm Jessica!"

"I was in the shadows, I saw what you did!"

"In the shadows, in the shadows, we're all in the shadows!"

"Can't I live with you, Anna? Anna, I love you, Anna!" he said, falling on the floor and writhing about.

"You stink, Clone. My husband is clean and good-looking. You're street trash."

"We're the same person!"

"You *were* the same person," she hissed, "for a few seconds, just as I was Jessica for a few seconds. Then I surpassed her, and now I am her, but you missed your chance, and I don't care. Commit suicide, live on the streets, I don't care!"

"Anna, I love you, Anna," Bob's clone sobbed. Anna the Clone pulled him to his feet and dragged him inside. Though much smaller Anna the Clone was by far stronger, she having eaten and slept properly since her birth, unlike Bob's clone. She shut the door and beat him about the head with her fists as he sobbed and begged her to stop and repeated that he loved her. She hit him over and over again, until, at last, he was silent. She stripped him naked and, sighing heavily, wrapped him in bin liner and dragged him to the shed. She hacked him to pieces and took them, with the clothes, to Jessica's car and stuffed them in the boot. Then she drove out into the countryside and slowly burnt the evidence in a metal bin, singing something about clean air and its effect on the soul.

Tenacity

Tenacity was the only virtue of Berta the pauper rope-weaver
But she did occasionally turn her hand to more complex issues
Like wearing a small ferret wedged onto a pole
And building the seventeen crutches for her seventeen children
Who all had severe inabilities to punctuate.
'Oh Jesus' little Amaretta would say, forgetting to add the exclamation
mark
Her words lacked all emphasis and she started to fade
While even smaller Jimmy would cry
'Who put the soup in my hollow wooden leg, who put the soup in my
hollow wooden leg,"
Forgetting the question mark, so no one answered him,
Which fuelled his belief that he was dead.
And so every day he used his soup-stained wooden leg to batter passing
tom cats
Who subsequently melted into mercury, which Jimmy then ate.
Thinking it would bring him back to life.
Ironically, it killed him.
His stomach swelled and burst and his younger, smaller sister,
Janine, tripped on the mess, being that she was blind,
And fell into a void created by mindless sex,
And when she landed the world had shrunk to the size of a prickly pear,
And she was God.
So poor Berta the pauper rope-weaver had to settle for
An invisible daughter, an exploded son, and God,
So she braided the rope until it could no longer fray,
And used it on her own dilapidated neck.

Arm

I swallow his fingers but forget to chop them off first and his arm juts out of my mouth nails in lung area and going lower, lips are almost at his armpit shoulder whichever you prefer but no gagging allowed, feel quite satisfactorily full up after dinner not too full it's just the right fit size four and a half please, he's wearing a shirt under a jumper sleeves not rolled up and button sleeve is tickling something down there it's comfortable his arm down my throat so we stay like that for a while but he brushes the lining of my stomach and he's crossed the line now but there's friction when you go the other way we're stuck and I can't help but wonder what that nice man in the shop will think when I go in and I've got an arm stuck in my mouth so he kisses the top of my head and then it's out.

Sex life

Fester yourself! Cried the boy and his tribe
And if it's a giraffe you want,
I'm a monsoon. But if you require a legitimate
Bonk, a moment of pensive thoughts permeate round

Father yourself! Cried the pen and a book
And if it's a menage you want,
I'm a baboon. But if you desire a laborious
Fool, a princeps or penchant twat elephant pound

Cover yourself! Cried the tin and the Sire
And if an obtuse member,
I am your man. But if you entice a mendacious
Old bitch, then open a door to a bastard who cares

Bugger yourself! Fried a bean in his pan
And emptily driven a barrel of snow,
Into new worlds. But demonstrate nothing if
You cannot become
A leather-bound armchair for two

Enema man! Cried a monk to a priest
They hopped to it quick style and shagged until dawn,
A rambunctious pair of ninnies I ever did see.
But twelve dozen pastries can wank over trees,
If I can just finish my pie.

The Octopus and The Barkeep

The octopus has its mind set on a bowl of rice for lunch. Steamed with shrimp. By god, he hated shrimp – alive. Dead, they were a treat, a feast for eyes, for stomach, for tentacles. So it was to be shrimp rice with a side of Miso soup.

"What do you think this is, Japan?" scoffed the bartender. "London? The inside of your squishy brain?"

"But, good sir-" began the octopus, but the barkeep would have none of it.

"None of that," he said, negotiating the bar to hustle the octopus. "None of your bullshit," he said, trying to push out all eight tentacles at once. "You'll have a drink or you'll have nothing at all."

"Fine," said the octopus sourly. "You induce a mood in me, some new sort of market ploy, ey? Got too much lemon juice, have you? Pah! You won't get me with that! I'll have a scotch."

"What do you think this is? Scotland? London? The inside-"

"Never mind! Never mind. What *do* you have, then, funny barkeeper man?"

"We have the usual!" he cried indignantly. "Pretzels, chips, apricot brandy, and Cinzano!"

"I'll have a Cinzano and chips."

"Very good, sir."

Despite his earlier resolve, the octopus felt he had made a fine choice and sat back to enjoy the ice-skating on the TV behind the bar. A rather attractive young ladybug was commentating. The octopus couldn't tell how many spots she had – her underbelly faced the camera – but he made a guess of five on each wing. As the barkeep poured the Cinzano, the octopus said:

"Hey – I'll make you a bet – I bet you that that ladybug yonder has five spots on each wing."

The barman said "Pah" and slammed the drink down. "If it's more than three I'll eat my hat." It was a rash statement, for he wore no hat. However the octopus had no chance to rejoinder as just then eleven shrimp piled into the bar. The barman smiled widely.

"Ladies! What'll it be today?"

As the barman saw to his regulars, the octopus was internally seething with anger. God, he hated live shrimp. But as his anger boiled, a plan was also forming.

When the shrimp were duly served, the octopus leant into the barkeeper and whispered, very, very quietly, "If I'm right, you've got to make them over there into shrimp rice for my lunch."

The bartender narrowed his eyes. "And if I win?"

"Name it."

"Four tentacles."

"Done."

The octopus' chips arrived but neither octopus nor bartender took any notice; both sets of eyes were fixated firmly on the screen. The ladybug eventually got up and walked over to the ice-skaters for an interview... She turned around... And then... There it was, for all to see. She had no spots at all! Not one. Not even a half. The bartender and the octopus smiled uncertainly at each other.

"Technically, I won," said the barman.

"Technically, you did," said the octopus sadly, as he looked at his poor tentacles and wondered which ones he'd miss least.

"But hey," said the barman, "It's not really on – I wouldn't feel right – it's like when you get a zero on the roulette, huh? Just buy another Cinzano and we'll call it quits, what do you say?"

"Splendid," said the octopus.

Double entrapment

She, fleeing from an unseen everything in a deserted, menacing hospital corridor, happens upon a monster who seems to offer her her liberty; and so she, unseeing, unsees, as he descends his volatile trap and encases her terrified head into it forever: perpetual entrapment, for all time her yellow eyes widened in total horror, a statue, living, feeling, not moving.

He, an atlas, with the strength to take on everything and bowing to nothing, with courage, stealth, and recklessness pursues her, his yellow blood pulsing through veins bulging out of pale, almost translucent skin; pulling her to him, he has her forever, his little doe, trapped once, trapped twice, and this time with nowhere to run and no saviour to come.

The Quest for Enormous Omelettes

Enormous omelettes for sale, it said. Enormous omelettes for sale. I thought, I've got to see this. What kind of a fool would advertise themselves in such a way? So I strapped on my bicycle clips and wheeled my way into the ghetto, where the shop was based. Yes, you could say I got mugged twice on my way there, but if you look at it optimistically they only took five quid and three of my teeth. And my bicycle clips, but they only wanted them 'cause they thought they were made out of titanium, when it should have been obvious that they were silver plastic. I got to the place a little after the watershed and felt safe swearing at the top of my voice when I saw that it was closed. Closed, and there in the window, taunting me, the advert again: 'Enormous omelettes for sale'. I threw a rock at the window but it didn't smash so I threw it again and it didn't smash again so I threw it again and it smashed. Then I ran away on my bike.

Hummhimmina's Tuft

It began like little tufts of grass, poking out of the barren field. A miracle, perhaps, or just the result of the previous season's extensive rainfall, for which all were very grateful. After a long drought and hunger, fields had sprung to life from nowhere, producing a harvest such as they hadn't seen in eighteen years of life, giving forth edible titbits and boilable broth ingredients and corn. That one field remained bare, but for the tufts, however; the earth stayed drier than July and harder than the giant nut that fell on old Martha's nose in the Year of the Nut and broke it clean off. The farmer whose field it was scratched his head whilst looking out at his field eleven times a day; he could be seen there at the exact same times every day, you could set your watch by him. He couldn't fathom why he had been chosen by his deity for such cruel punishment. His daughter, however, a ten year old with the wisdom of an old man and the simplicity of a fool, had other ideas, and had secretly been watering the patch where the tuft grew with her special blend of water from the well, infused with stolen petals from their richer neighbour's fertile land, and her cat's urine. As her father was scratching his head for the ninetieth day in a row, and the congealed blood on the wound there began to flow freely again, Hummhimmina, for so she was called, screamed with shock and delight. For there, in the corner of her father's barren field, where he couldn't espy her, Hummhimmina had found that her watered patch was sprouting her very own little tuft of grass.

She ran full pelt to her little stone house, tripping on her way and obtaining a lovely read welt along her forehead, and she ran clean through the door, which was, luckily, open. Her mother, Hemmhimmino, whacked her on the shin with a stirring spoon for her clumsiness, and asked nothing about her scream, for Hummhimmina was always screaming about something. Hummhimmina sulked for forty-five seconds, then took a bucket and ran to the well to make up some more of her special life-giving mixture. Having collected the water, the petals,

171

and her cat's wee, she gently poured the lot over the tuft of grass and sang it an encouraging song, that went:

> grow little tufty, grow fro grow
> and if you don't, I won't water you again
> grow little tufty-wuft, grow-y fro-y grow
> and then I'll be a rich girl and run away from home
>
> grow tufty wufty tuft, grow until you're grown
> or I won't be nice to you and you won't be alive
> grow my little tufty friend, come out and play
> and then Daddy will see that I'm better than James

James was Hummhimmina's little brother who their father doted on. He was only eleven months old but his father had already named him heir to the farm and announced that he would grow to be a hero. Hummhimmina had her reservations, which was fair enough, given his size and the fact that all he did was cry and poo into his nappy, and didn't feel too kindly towards the family's new edition. As she sang her song she elaborated on all the things that would happen if the plant grew well - fame for her, maybe a little more love, the chance of a better life, perhaps - and on all the things that would happen if it didn't grow well - which are best left between Hummhimmina and the plant.

Each day the tufts grew an inch longer and taller and looked thicker and healthier. After several weeks they were so long that they'd begun to droop over with the force of gravity, and the whole thing was wider than Hummhimmina's torso, top to bottom. She decided the plant needed a name and she called it Hessikinto, which she later shortened to Kinto so that it'd fit better into her songs of growth. She could feel the crackle of something magical surrounding Kinto and she couldn't wait to find out what was going to happen with it. Would it be a giant carrot? Giant magic carrots, maybe? She thought she'd give Kinto another week and then it would be time to dig him out. Each night as her parents cooed over James and either snubbed or whacked her with whatever implement they happen to have in their easy reach, Hummhimmina merely smiled dreamily and thought about Kinto and what he'd turn out to be and how much he'd be worth. James could gurgle or scream for all she cared, *he* didn't have a secret plant growing right under her father's big ugly nose.

The morning for digging up Kinto arrived murky and cold and Hummhimmina was mighty glad of the dull weather, which would all the better hide her secret activities. As usual her father got up, marvelled over his son, and set off for a day of standing in his field, wondering what to do and what had gone wrong. Once he'd gone Hummhimmina performed her morning chores and then escaped her mother's watch by prodding James and making him bawl. She slipped out and ran to Kinto with her little shovel and a very large sack to put him in, which earlier that morning she'd stolen from their rather empty larder. She knelt down and jabbed her shovel into the earth, coming up with a nice little shovel-full, which she flung behind her. She did it again, and heard a noise. "Whosat, whosere?" she cried, standing up, brandishing her shovel around like a dagger at the empty mist. A muffled cry replied, "Hmm hmm mm ma!" Hummhimmina gasped and fell down onto her knees before Kinto. She brushed aside his thick tufts and there, just visible above the earth and beneath his tufts, a hard, round surface was peeking out, like a very, very big potato. Hummhimmina rapped at it with her knuckles and it cried out again, "Hmm hmm mm ma!" Hummhimmina figured out that Kinto wasn't ready to be dug out yet and so, casting aside the shovel, she knelt before him and sang him her new favourite song.

> Kinto, Kinto, Kinto, I love you,
> Kinto you're my friend and I love you very much
> Kinto, Kinto, Kinto, I love you,
> Kinto you're my friend and I love you very much

One week later, Hummhimmina was wondering again whether or not she ought to dig Kinto out. But as she sat with him and bent down to kiss his potato-like protrusion, she saw something new; the tops of two eyes were now peeking out, and they were looking right at her. "Kinto!" she cried. "You have eyes!" Once again, all Kinto would reply was "Hmm hmm mm ma!" In another week, both of his eyes were entirely above the earth and, while they fixated mostly on Hummhimmina while she was there, when she wasn't they roamed the plane of earth before them, looking for the first time at the world, and thinking how very dull it was. Kinto was very bored of the earth in another week's time, when the top of his nose appeared; and a month after that, when his mouth was nearing the surface, and he'd begun to pick up the rudiments of language in his mind but couldn't speak yet, he willed himself to emerge quicker. In another month his whole face was out.

"Hummhimmina," he said one morning as she watered him. "Can't I have a cheese like you? I wish I could taste something!"

"Alright," she said, suppressing her natural greed and unwillingness to share. And indeed the following week she regretted ever giving Kinto food to eat, for, as well as wanting an equal share of Hummhimmina's food, which wasn't generous anyway, he was much bigger than her and began demanding more and more.

"Hummhimmina, I'm starving!" he'd wail, tears pouring down his huge face which Hummhimmina would have to wipe away with her skirt. "Please feed me more, it hurts!" and she'd have to hoard whatever she could, steal whenever she could, and go without herself in order to feed the ever-hungry Kinto. But no matter how much she fed him, he grew no more, and remained for the next three months only head out of the ground. Whatever was underneath the ground attached to the head stayed there. At the end of the three months Hummhimmina was looking peaky, thin, and pale with malnutrition, and was weak and injured from the many beatings she'd received for stealing food. One day she woke up and sat down meekly at the table where her parents were eating their meagre breakfasts. An empty plate stood at Hummhimmina's place. As she sat down and looked in puzzlement at the offending item, her father growled:

"No more food for you."

"What, Papa?" she cried.

"You're a thief. No more food until you stop stealing."

Hummhimmina started wailing. Her father had expected that and ignored her, tucking into his own hunk of dry bread. But when she didn't stop when he had drained the very last drop of his muddy oat drink, he kicked her under the table and said:

"Shut up."

"Please Papa. You don't understand. I had to steal that food. I stole it for Kinto!"

"Eh? Kinto? Is that another stray cat you've picked up? Because if it is..." he shook his fist at her.

"No! Just - just come and see," she said, putting her little hand in his and dragging him away from the table. He followed her to the tufty patch, Hemmhimmino close behind with James. Kinto's eyes saw them coming from afar and he began to sweat with fear. As they approached Hummhimmina's father's eyes widened in amazement.

"What is this, Hummhimmina?" he asked, kneeling to stroke the tufts of grass that were Kinto's hair.

"That's where all the food's been going," she said, crying. "That's Kinto."

Kinto looked up at Hummhimmina's father with pleading, scared eyes.

"He's a miracle," her father said. "Can he speak?"

"Yes - go on, Kinto."

"Hello," Kinto said nervously. "I'm Kinto. Sorry I ate all your food. I was really hungry. Have you got any more?"

Hummhimmina's father frowned. "Afraid we've had a bad year, son. We're all but broke. I wasn't planning on telling Hummhimmina yet, but... We've got to go away. Find another farm or another fortune, else we'll starve."

"Hummhimmina, don't leave me!" Kinto cried. Hummhimmina dropped to the floor and embraced Kinto's larger-than-life head.

"I won't!" she swore.

"There's no other way, Hummhimmina. We have no crops to sell. Unless we have something to sell, we starve."

"Sell her," Hemmhimmino said, jiggling James around. "Old Martha needs someone around the house. She hasn't been too able since her nose came off. She'll pay a good price for Hummhimmina, I'll warrant."

"No! Not old Martha!" Hummhimmina cried, but her father was already looking at her like she was a bag of money.

"Yes," he said slowly, advancing towards her. "It'd only be a few years, she's old, and without her nose she won't last much longer. Come on, my girl, to Old Martha's!"

"I won't, I won't!" Hummhimmina cried, throwing herself on the floor.

"Come, come, you don't want Kinto to starve, do you?"

"Of course not! But who'll look after him when I've gone?"

"Well I will, won't I? He's my crop, I've got to look after him."

"He's not a crop! He's Kinto!"

"He's a miracle, my girl, and we must keep him alive!"

"I won't go to old Matha's!"

"Not even for poor little Kinto?"

Hummhimmina looked at Kinto, who looked at her.

"Yes, for Kinto."

So that afternoon her father marched her round to the noseless old Martha and exchanged her for a sum of money healthy enough to keep he and his family fed and clothed until the following year. Hummhimmina was slave-driven by old Martha and never got the opportunity to visit her beloved Kinto. The years dragged by and Hummhimmina spent long days cleaning, cooking, mending, and tending to Martha, while her girlhood passed her by, and, before she knew it, she was a young lady, ripe for marriage. She often thought about Kinto, who she thought fondly back on as her best friend, the lover she was cruelly taken from, her only chance of a future, and awaited him. As she eased out of childhood into womanhood, and began to lose the ability to accept as fact mystical or impossible things, however, Kinto evolved in her memory from a giant plant into a strong, wild boy that her family took in, and it was for him that she waited. But she knew she could never leave until old Martha passed on, and every night she prayed for her death. Her wish was granted on the eve of Hummhimmina's eighteenth birthday. Finally free, she happily took the money old Martha had left her on her death bed and made the long trek back to her parents' old farm. But when she got there, it was deserted and derelict. All signs of life, including Kinto, were gone. Hummhimmina cried and cried, her dreams all dashed against the wayside, and ran around her old house maniacally. When she'd expended all her energy doing that she lay down and slept for twelve hours. Awaking in the morning she decided she was going to forget Kinto, not waste any more years of her life waiting for him to rescue her, and make it on her own.

And so she did. Aged twenty-eight, she'd found a decent husband and had children of her own, whom she called Hessakimlo and Hessalimto. They were twin boys, good as a pair of eagles, and stocky too; Hummhimmina's pride but also her demise. She made a good mother and was full of love to give but her mind had been blighted by sorrow since the day she found out Kinto was no longer at her farm. When her boys grew into men and her husband had passed on, she knew she had to find Kinto before her own death, lest she miss her chance to pursue true joy. Not really know where to start, she headed back to the old family farm and, to her intense surprise and delight, found someone living there.

"Ho!" she called to the man digging in a field. "Ho, who are you?"

The man looked up and replied "I be James, this be my farm, and you be trespassing so Miss better go afore I introduce my shovel to her head."

"Can it really be, James, my long-lost brother, son of my proud father John and our mother Hemmhimmino?"

"That be me...You're never Hummhimmina? They said you's dead."

"I, dead? No James, I'm here and alive and I came back to find...my family. Where are our parents?"

"They's dead, int they?"

"Dead, really?"

"Oh yes, very dead, these ten year."

"And what of the...what of my...what of Kinto?"

"Him? He be upstairs, int he?"

"Upstairs? What - in the house, here?"

"Oh yes, in the house, here."

Hummhimmina ran to the house, through the door (again, thankfully open), and up the stairs. She fell into her old room, which was empty, bounded into her parents' room, which was also empty, and finally tried James' room, which was occupied.

"Kinto, Kinto, oh my, oh my Kinto!" she cried, espying the enormous head peeking out of the bed. She flung herself at his side. "Kinto! It's your Hummhimmina, come back!"

"Hummhimmina's dead, they said."

"Yet here I am, alive!"

"She's dead, they said. You got any cheese?"

"Not changed a drop! Oh my Kinto, here I am, Hummhimmina, come back for you!"

"She's dead. Cheese?"

"Kinto, my Kinto, don't you understand, I'm not dead, I'm here, here, for my Kinto!"

"Can't be, Hummhimmina died."

She punched his large head. "It's me, Hummhimmina, here!"

"A ghost!" Kinto cried, shrinking into his bed. "James, a ghost! James, help!"

James came bounding up the stairs.

"Come on, idiot, she be Hummhimmina, alive, not ghost."

"Ghost, James, Hummhimmina's ghost has come!"

"Shut *up*, idiot," James said, bringing down the shovel that was still in his hand heavily on Kinto's leg. "She be alive and here."

"Cheese?" Kinto asked. Hummhimmina looked between the two men in disgust.

"What's wrong with you two? James, why do you hit him? Kinto, why are you in bed?"

"He be ill, int he? He be a right freak, don't he? James be always looking after him, don't I?"

"Why do you talk like that? Why do you hit him?"

"Talk how? He be a right idiot, that's why. Never be helping, always be wanting cheese. I be breaking my back for him, and he just be bleating all the day long!"

"Cheese, who has cheese for me?"

Hummhimmina's expression of incredulity and disappointment and disgust was lost on her brother and Kinto.

"I think I'll go now."

"That be the best, Hummhimmina."

"Bring cheese next time, Hummhimmina!"

"Farewell, my brothers."

Hummhimmina turned and left. Before leaving the farm entirely she visited the spot of Kinto's birth and found it, along with the rest of the farm, sprouting potatoes and cabbage. A forlorn-looking cow was sitting in the old barn. Hummhimmina spat on the ground and left.

Gods...

It's when I walk down the street with my ears open that I think the world must be in harmony with itself.

GIRL TO HER FRIEND: ...it was pretty huge....

A SECOND LATER, A WOMAN TO HER COLLEAGUE: ...I mean, it's not fair, is it? I'm doing the work and not getting paid.

A FINAL PAIR OF GIRLS, GIGGLING: ...for a penis enlargement!

I was meandering along, a destination in mind but not a path, humming a melody of my own creation, thinking: "God, am I God? Are we all gods in our own right? Did I create their harmony, or did they create mine? But who created the creator?", and darkness passed over my face, and I shrivelled into a miserable being.

The woman holding the fireball

She was standing in the middle of the road, and it was night. I was watching through the window of my front room. The street itself was silent, or it seemed so to me – I felt that there was no other person in the world but me and her. She was staring at the moon, which was, that night, three-quarters full, and enormous – I'd never seen it so close to the earth. It was incredibly windy out there – I could hear the howling in my chimney, and her purple dress was billowing out everywhere, the sashes around her whipping up, slapping the sky. But the ball of fire that she held aloft in her hand was impervious to the terror of the wind. She looked calm, but terrible. I was petrified, rigid.

I had felt her presence when I was innocently preparing my dinner in the kitchen. Lights on, oven warming the room, yet a freezing dark feeling enveloped me. I hadn't wanted to believe she was there. I forced myself to continue chopping vegetables, but my hands were betraying me, shaking a little then uncontrollably, and I was a danger to myself. I tried to fill the kettle, but it dropped to the floor with a huge crash, water all over the floor. That's when I slowly took myself into the front room, creeping around the door, not bothering to turn the lights on in here, for what good would that do? Unnatural light could not dispel the unnatural darkness emanating from her. And I saw her immediately, anyway: the fireball in her hand lighting herself, the street, into my house.

A few years of the wasteland

She wouldn't testify to the homicide but she did categorise my fish:
The ephemeral fish, a-wandering through the desert plains,
bleating like lost souls trying to find meaning in food.
'If he has some, I'm having a canvas-bag full of horse shit' one announced,
and in agreement another leapt up and smacked a boy on the buttocks.
The boy stared on in pure bewilderment.
His mother, seeing the cacophony of evil brewing beneath the smiles
of merchant's pimpled faces,
hauled his ruddy backside up and threw him in his cage
(shared with pet marsupials).
A trumpet sounded and the race began.
Thirty thousand eggs jumped on the backs of cockerels
and whipped them till a thick layer of cockroach skins
plastered the floor and made for poor footing.
Disappointed, three men clad in Hawaiian shirts took out their machetes
and started lopping off limbs at random.
The third, the cruellest and most arbitrary,
started with his own foot to show how serious he was,
and not more than three decades later the area known as Legland
was a haven for the more daring tourists
or those with a penchant for absolute *schadenfreude*:
pleasure at seeing one's companion's arm lopped off
as she holds out a peseta to a starving child.
The moon shone down orange on a beaten up tramp enjoying the spectacle quietly
from a disused army bunker where he stored jars of blood
and nail clippings to sell to scientists for a small sum;
he was saving to buy a razor blade to slit his wrists
and jump into the nearby lake where they said paradise awaited those

who gave up their earthly bodies to it.
Having achieved his goal several weeks later the tramp,
far from the paradise he craved, was raised up on a dais on the sand,
pulled along by snakes driven by fire and fury,
destined to spin forever in a cloudy night.
It was 3 'o' clock.
A haggard child crawled by on its belly calling 'slaughter! slaughter!'
After this, nothing else was known – except that a few greasy slabs of
horse meat
were seen with a priest, fuelling the next great scandal,
which I'll tell you about after supper.

Moonblind from the male to the female

So many men keep ungulates in secret sheds that a dozen such men's angry wives came to lay a siege around the soldier's quarters atop the craggy hill, with around a hundred condors armed with machetes, all doped up with a bolus of ether, ejaculating over anyone nearby. Tetley, a man of moderate means, took his seventeen-tipped columbium knife, made originally for his wife's kitchen, for he wanted to use it as a weapon. But he was moonblind, and the Women's Statutes outlawed fighting for the non-sighted. However, it wasn't the knife; its oblong handle of rubber resembled the feel of banana-skin, so a banana he took. Not only was he a fool, you see, but a junkie as well. With some cheap bronco and his banana, the pimpled man's thoughts focussed on one thing alone: 'Steal'.

♂

My drone became louder, a braver man would have killed himself, but the mobile army said not a thing: this is how we were, you see. He was almost upon the women, but as that wife of mine looked up she succeeded in spotting him and fired at he who almost killed her, then kicked his carcass for egg-filled laughter. On the rim of their siege but not beyond sight, a type of spliced man-and-beast or man-beast roared and rendered the blowsy controllable, if not submissive then pacified. Soon, this half-goat, withered, hungry and old, is trying to plead with the bronzed harpies for a peace treaty of a year, or the compromise to adhere magnanimously to our andante lives; but they all went defibrillatory and inscribed the goat-man's title in the come of a toad and made him eat turnips. Meanwhile, beneath the barricade, my now flabbergasted comrades flicked ants and greased the pole for a whole year – and so on

♀

His drone made me fury. Brave, maybe, but he couldn't kill; barely mobile, armed with a banana, this drunkard junkie was so pathetic you almost felt sympathy; but as his wife was a friend of mine we succeeded in shooting him down. They fired at us, who then could fail to retaliate? For dinner we had egg-filled bowls, rimmed with sugar, sweet but bitter, and all types of woman spliced together, timid, boisterous, blowsy, dominant or controllable; and if the men did not vacate the area soon, their goats would be burnt. It is trying, to see them plead with us, offering the bronze they hadn't yet found. This continued for a year, until they agreed to adhere to our andante rules. We went crazy, we defibrillated our hearts, we took their titles and sang: "Fly vixen! Come toad! Live in our abode!" Turnips banished to beneath the earth, my diet now flabbergasted the ants' legal representative and we climbed poles and swam all day – I this day, I flummox, I beat on the walls, but vacuumed earplugs couldn't shut out a thought: these people, then, these women on mountains who claim to propound freedom, who we treat as dogs, don't see things as we do. I'm about to take a gun, then, on the last day, when there came along the right honourable goblin-lord who was once man's friend; he was carrying his hat, and suddenly, we knew we were saved.

shouted and I sang, but I no longer needed earplugs; we were a people then, of interminable mountainous joy. We rode rapids, we came to propound anarchy, we treated the men as dogs, and I don't see we're doing wrong. I'm finally happy, then, when one day there came along a righteous looking goblin, defending the men as friends, and he was forceful and cruel, and suddenly, we knew we were ruined.

Distance and its loves

It was seventy years from now
I'd taken the time to find a flaw
In all you did and more
And air travel prices had rocketed high
So I couldn't get out to Jamaica.

A poor little broken boy out from the shadows
Said, 'Mister can you spare me a quid?'
I gave him a fiver, he cried and I said,
'Now come child, here is your maker.'

That said I punched his pathetically small
Nose and broke it in one go
Then I smacked him about and in one final blow
I plunged my knife into his chest.

'Thank God I was here,' I said,
'If I'd been someone else,
I'd have told him to leave me alone.'

That done I continued along Augustine Walk
With a pen in my pocket and a leaf in my shoe
Praising the sky and the sea and the blue
For keeping me so far from you.

The Most Impenetrable Place

<u>Part 1</u>

"Most impenetrable," the sign reads, pointing towards the door to my right. Since I'm being chased by my boyfriend, whom I've only just discovered is in league with the creature of the sea – the thing that emerged from the uprising blobs and acquired consciousness, and a desire to see me dead – I'm glad to see it. Impenetrable is the way I like my hide-outs to be. I let myself in (assuming the place becomes impenetrable after the one in need enters, of course), and find myself faced with a small boy. He greets me, and his colouring and accent suggest he comes from India, but there is something odd about his eyes.

"You're staring at my eyes, aren't you?" he asks.

Startled, I reply – "Are you blind?"

"It was my mother's idea," he says, and then I see it: where his eyes should be are not eyes, but tattoos of eyes. And not normal eyes, either – cat's eyes, blue.

"This is how I used to look," he says, handing me a photograph. In it he has large brown eyes.

"But...why?"

"My mother said it would make me more employable."

"To whom?" I ask, aghast.

"Her Royal Majesty, Queen Katherine XIV."

For the first time, I see beyond the boy and discover there is a regal-looking suite behind him. He hurries off to prepare a huge bed-like seat. There is a man beside it, watching, waiting. He is dark-featured and handsome. When the seat is ready, he turns to me and says, "Come on then, my queen, the show's about to begin."

"What?" I take a step back and do not bump into the door. Turning around, I see the room has become vast, and there is a stage where I thought there was a wall.

"Who are you? Where am I? I thought —"

"My love, I am Jareth, King of the Goblins, and you are my Queen, Katherine XIV, and if we do not sit soon, we shall keep everyone waiting."

I look to his left and right and see that we are in the middle of an audience, whose faces had hitherto been obscured, because the only lights in the house are on our suite, in the centre of the audience.

I sit down and watch a play which retells the story of mine and Jareth's union.

It was in the days that the country had no unified rule. Rich men, tyrants and bastards ruled motley bunches in disparate lands, and those who just wanted to live a peaceful life had to toil until their backs broke, to keep the rulers off them. Jareth, in those days, led the Goblins in the rocky mountains, in the east. He often fought with the nearby gangs – the Angels, the Dogs, the Bastards, and others – and every leader desired nothing so much as to extend their power. I belonged to a very poor family working the land for Jareth, but I was headstrong, and arrogant, and I refused to spend my life working like my parents. I stole away one night, at the age of fifteen, and headed up, up, up into the mountains where I knew, somewhere, Jareth lived. Through trickery, wile, and cunning I snuck into his inner lair, a pool of water surrounded by steep rocks, where the older boys, the most cherished members of his gang, played after a battle. At the top, Jareth's home. At the bottom of the rocks I hid behind some bushes, but the boys there were more observant than the guards in the outer regions, and I was caught. Angry and petulant, I struggled in my bonds as I was brought before Jareth. Before he could give the command to have me killed, I shouted that I wanted to join his gang. He laughed coldly, but saw some sport to be had, and told me that if I want to join, I must mug a mugger. And not just any, the most fearsome and feared in the land. This man wore a gold locket, a relic of the lover he murdered in unfounded jealousy, and was the only thing he would not put a price on.

I stole that locket, took it back to Jareth, and was admitted to the Goblins. He took the locket from me with a smile, and kissed my lips. In the kiss he poured his breath into me, and I had to breathe it all in, the final test. From that moment on, I became his lover, and with my power combined with his, the Goblins became untouchable. There the story closes on stage, but I feel that something is missing, that the story lacks its proper ending, but as I can't remember why I think that, I simply smile at my lover and let him caress me.

As the actors leave the stage, a nurse brings my son to me, though it is only now that I remember I have one. He had lots of blond hair and a few baby teeth. I take him and, cuddling him, announce proudly to the room, "I made him myself". Everyone applauds, and Jareth looks at me fondly. I feel very strange, suddenly. I look at Jareth. He is wearing a jacket just like the one my father used to wear. "My father…" I say slowly, and then I realise – Jareth does not own a jacket like that – but I'd described it to him once, when I was missing my father – and I know this is not real, I am in a fiction, and I need to leave immediately. I jump up, shove the baby in Jareth's arms, and, thus encumbered, he cannot chase me as I flee the room, running through the first door I find.

I'm in the castle gardens, and it's daylight. Not wanting to wait to find out if what's behind me can give chase, I hurry through the vast, elegant grounds. I pass a gang of wolves devouring a carcass. Some of them have shiny black coats, but most of them are mangy with patchy fur. They look up as I pass but either recognise me or are too busy with their meal to care. I run past them and only stop when my heart is on fire. I rest by a tree and try to right my thoughts: what really happened with Jareth and I?

Part 2

I'm brown-haired and blue eyed. I'm talking to my little daughter, asking her questions about me. I ask her if she thinks I'm pretty. She says, yes, very. I tell her she'll look like us when she's grown – she has my eyes. She squeals and says she hopes so. She says daddy is one of the prettiest. He has double sleep, she says. I ask her what she means. She says it's when you sleep half the night, get up and tend to the special flowers that need watering at a specific time of night – suddenly I have an image of him, in an underground room somewhere tending to the flowers, the beautiful pink flowers, as he kisses their petals – and then go to bed for the rest of the night.

Her image is so naïve and beautifully innocent, but as I sit back, I am reminded of a room – an indoor tropical garden, where I sat on a bench watching the semi-naked women jog around the paths between the flowers, wondering if I was destined to be one of them, or whether I was one of them already. As I sat there, I pondered to myself fretfully: 'Can I ask him to renounce sorcery, or are we not yet close enough for that? If I ask, will he suspect me?'

He has creatures of terror in his power; flying monkeys with claws, which swoop down on a different town once a week and pluck someone from the market square, and carry them away, for who knows what purpose. It had been rumoured that they only take the biggest men, a symbol of their power, or of his, but in one town I hid, on the day of the steal, and watched from the shadows as they took a small girl. But if they do not hold the market, how can they trade, and eat, and live?

Now he controls not just the creatures, but the elements. I have been running from him, hiding from him for so long I can't remember how many days it has been, or whether I should be counting days, or weeks, or months. In the town I hide today, we the townspeople see from the distance a tidal wave engulf a whole coastal town. We are not afraid for ourselves – we know he only attacks one town at a time, and usually those that are most resistant, and my current town is painfully submissive – but we watch, horrified, knowing that the sea will claim all the lives in that place. In my mind's eye I see them try to outrun it. I can see myself there with my parents, blissfully unaware that the tide is coming in unnaturally quickly. I can see us drowning together, and am bemused that this bestows on me a sense of contentedness, as well as a feeling of terror.

When the sea has receded, no-one in the nearby town in which I am hiding will go there. After many such rescue attempts on devastated places, all resulting in a second wave killing the would-be rescuers, which we all knew should be physically impossible, those nearby would not set foot in the perished place. But I have to go there, simply because no-one else can.

When I reach the beach I see a creature sitting on a wet rock, tossing a stone back and forth between its slimy hands. The creature is shrunken and deformed, and, it seems, gleeful. I sneak up on it and grab the stone. Before the creature or I have time to register surprise, the stone becomes a key which unlocks a portal to the castle. Immediately I know I've fallen for his trick; but I'd expected one, there's always the chance of a trick around every corner, and though I am scared, I am also almost excited. What will he do to me? At the entrance to the castle, the huge double oak doors I know so well, I am not surprised to find them open at my slightest touch. I walk through, and it is deathly quiet inside – which metaphor I find quite accurate, as I enter the vast dining hall and find the guests at the party I have gate-crashed slumped, dead, over their dinner plates. But no sooner do I realise they are corpses than I see them all sit up at once and look at me, falling about laughing. And I realise this was the trick: I'm still on the beach, the key-stone did not transport me to the castle, but fuelled the hallucination, and tricked me within the trick. I smile at his sense of humour, despite everything. "You do it to yourself," I say aloud, and bash out the brains of the creature with the slimy hands, with its own key-stone.

I should have recognised it as a hallucination. He's played a similar trick on me before, but it was a memory then, and the difference in perspective was sufficient for me not to realise. It was when I was visiting Malign Isle, as it came to be known. Once a populated place, now it was empty since the inhabitants had fled in fear of a mystical, eerie, malign presence that had been terrorising the people. It was said to live in the tall, white-leaved pine trees that were unique to this island. I felt drawn there by some pull I could not place, as I did to every place that was devastated, one way or another, by his force. At night I went there and found a group of ten people stuck there; the boats had all left, and these poor souls had been forgotten. At night they would huddle together for protection; a larger group of them encircling a smaller one, encircling a single person. They told me there had been many more of them left behind, but every few nights someone would disappear. They did not know me, but in an act of generosity I was unaccustomed to, took me into their circle and gave me the centre position for the night. I felt safe in there and fell asleep. As soon as I dropped off, I felt the ground leave my feet and my perspective change, and I was transported to the castle. But, unlike the hallucination, I saw not from my own perspective, but from his, and I knew he was feeding me a memory. His memory. I saw him walk slowly, deliberately, as if injured, away from the castle and towards a desolate place. He was panting, and I felt the pain in his stomach – the injury was there, and I knew this was not long after the most fateful day, when he had been almost fatally hurt. He climbed painfully up a hill, over which was a ramshackle building, as ugly and neglected as the castle was grandiose and loved. I recognised it the moment we caught glimpse of it. The guard on the door fearfully stepped aside as he approached. Inside, it was dark, dank, filthy. Two other guards were standing with their backs to the entrance. He saw from their body language that they were arguing, and hung back to eavesdrop.

"She's weakening! She might be dying! We've got to do something!"

"She left, didn't she? She deserves it!"

"She sacrificed her freedom to spare our lives!"

"So she's weak."

"That's not weakness! We've got to tell him what she did!"

He staggered out. Grabbing the guard at the door, he hissed:

"Release her tonight. If you tell a soul I was here, there will be no help for you."

As the memory faded, I woke realising I'd discovered why he freed me. I jumped up and broke the circle. The others woke and shrieked in fear as I did so, thinking we were under attack.

And then we were.

A large, human-like figure emerged from the darkness. In the half-light of the stars and the moon it seemed to be an approximation of a human, a waxwork, maybe, or a plasticine figure. It had holes for eyes and mouth, and lumps for ears and nose.

"Give me a weapon," I said, and someone handed me a spear. I hurled it, and the figure swatted it out of the way. It in turn hurled a dagger at me. I dodged it, but heard it connect with someone behind me.

"Drop your weapons and run!" I commanded. I heard them obey and snatched up a discarded spear. It swatted this away too. We exchanged throws, me dodging, it swatting, and I knew it was better than me. I was panicked; no human but Jareth could have beaten me at this, but this was not human, and, quite likely, was created by Jareth. My momentary lapse ended the fight. A dagger struck into my chest. I started bleeding heavily, and dropped to one knee. At this, the figure changed its demeanour; it seemed concerned, and hesitantly crept forward, as if to see what damage it'd done. In pain and gasping, I could not stop it from approaching, but, seeing a chance, I exaggerated my broken stance. When it was upon me, I pulled the dagger from my chest and chopped off its hand, then its head. The head rolled, defunct, onto the ground.

I collapsed onto the ground too. The other people slowly crept back to me, unsure of their safety.

"It's OK," I panted. "It's gone. Bloodmoss," I said. Someone passed me a handful, and I staunched my wound. "I have big breasts," I said by way of explanation, and lost consciousness.

Part 3

"Stop," I say, and the actors obey. "Where is the comedy?" I'm tired of this tragic story. Immediately they rush around, changing costume, impeccable. The lights change from black-red to green-yellow. A lone man takes the stage with his grotesque comedy mask on.

"Where is my lunch?" he demands, gesturing wildly. "Where did that damn servant girl put *my lunch*?"

The audience are giggling - the plate of lunch is dangerously close to his feet, on the floor - and after several near misses, he steps right in it. Half the audience bellow, and the other half squirm uncomfortably: everyone knows a foot in the lunch is a euphemism for cunnilingus.

In the next scene, the offending servant girl is being taken to a brothel which is located in an underground car park, and is named "Bucolic". All of the whores, male and female, line up on one side of the stage, and the madam, a woman whose lower half is swirling and blue, perhaps a genie or a mermaid, stands on the other.

"How do they get her legs to look like that?" I marvel.

It is no ordinary brothel. The clients cannot choose their whores; rather the madam, every time a new client comes in, searches in their mind, and chooses the whore most complementary to their ways of thinking, but it seems to have nothing to do with sex. Not complementary sexual desires, but complementary powers, and from this is engendered incomparable sex. It seems to me her talent is wasted. Why pair people up based on power, I think, only for them to have sex? With this, wars could be won! But as soon as the thought escapes into my consciousness, I confuse myself. Since when did sex and war become two separate things to me? I am sex, I am war!

As if reading my thoughts, he leans in to me.

"How do witches fly?" he whispers. "What is their speed and accuracy?"

I can't see but I know there is a sardonic smile on his lips. One that used to seduce me, now puts me on my guard.

"Here is the marriage of sex and war," I whisper back. He stops smiling, he realises he's used the same weapon against me in two different battles, and in that instant I know I've won this time. He sits back, and I leave calmly and erect.

There are snakes on the floor in the hall outside, but I've never feared their paltry venom. Something down there stirs; I thought it was an asp. And then I think, "But by God, I must find Friedreich Fred!"

He was an astronomer. The greatest in the world, we believed. After the fall of all he stayed loyal to his only master, the sky. I knew he would go back to his observatory and live there divining whatever people pay him to in order to live his galaxial life, and there I find him. He doesn't leave his post, as I come in. Many minutes pass, and I wait for him to finish his observation. Very slowly he backs away from the telescope.

"Never, in all my life," he says, full of schoolboy awe, and grinning in the same manner. "I filmed it, too. Look."

He takes me over to a computer, and plays me the marvel. I see the blackness of space, dotted by the indomitable stars and galaxies. In the midst of the regular darkness, which I would call black, something blacker emerges, round and raging. It pelts towards our star at great speed, but when still some distance away, it stops and roars, burns, next to it, a black hole, or black sun, I don't know which.

"What is it?" I ask.

"I don't know!" he cries gleefully. "I don't know!" And he hurries back to his looking-post, and I know I'll get nothing more from him until he does.

I sit in silence on the great hill outside, just beyond the walls of the observatory. I watch the night sky, revelling in the passion I know Friedreich Fred feels for this ineffable place. I'm jealous that my sympathy for his lifelong love is fleeting. I watch the moon. Suddenly, I see something pass over it.

"Friedreich!" I shout. He doesn't stir. The moment passes; I can hear my breathing hitched my throat. I see another one. "Friedreich!" I shout again. I hear him galloping over. "I've just seen the silhouettes of two witches pass over the moon," I gasp.

Wordlessly we attend to the moon. We watch a red shadow cover the moon, slowly, with so much less haste and more clarity than the witches, flowing in the same direction as the witches.

"Aphids," he says.

"What-"

"-they move on semitransparent red leaves," he interrupts. "They're as big as us. They must be following the witches." His schoolboy awe-grin is replaced by wonder, curiosity, and a little fear. "Something big is occurring," he says. "And since it must be tied into your doings, it's better if you don't know what."

I'm prepared to take his advice, and we make frenetic love on the Observatory Hill. Our farewell gift to each other.

Part 4

One day I was sitting, staring into a river running wild, when a boy, panting, ran down to meet me.

"He's hurt," he said.

"Go away." I did not look at the boy.

"It's your fault. Come on! He's asking for you!"

"My fault? *My* fault?"

"Yes, yours, and yours alone! You never should have left!"

I turned, incredulous, to this presuming young boy. "What are you talking about?"

"It was all a trick! They made him think you had to leave; they knew he was invincible with you, but they feared you and envied you; they knew that without you he was weak, that he would let his guard down! When you went, he became weaker and weaker, until he couldn't fight like he used to. And then they attacked!"

"He was betrayed?"

"By those he trusted most. Please, you must come. We can't save him."

Grabbing my bag, I jumped to my feet and ran, and ran.

He groaned. He could not speak. A crashing sound, and then I burst in. I took one look at his bloodied clothes and dropped to my knees.

"Don't speak," I ordered, and leant into his wound. I cupped my hands around the hole in his stomach, and lowered my mouth to it. The watchers watched in awe as I sucked the metal intruder out of his stomach, into my mouth. As soon as it was in I spat it out, and pulled a mass of green stuff from my bag, and plugged the gaping, bleeding hole.

"Bloodmoss," I whispered. "Sleep."

I ushered the watchers out of the room, and obediently they followed.

"I guard here. You three keep watch outside." They looked uncertainly at each other. "You heard my orders! Go!" Reluctantly the three filed out, and I stood by the side of the doorway, eyes and ears standing to every attention there could be.

Over 24 hours passed and the blue-eyed boy tentatively snuck back in. He passed me a plate of food. I put it on the floor, untouched, un-looked at.

When he returned, I was still standing, and the food was rotting. He took the plate away and returned with another. The next day he replaced that too, and, hesitating near the door, asked:

"Have you slept?"

"No."

"This whole time"

"Has it been long?"

"Three days!"

I shrugged. "He and I are as one. If he sleeps, I don't need to."

The boy seemed struck by these words, and left, this time taking all the food.

On the fourth day, he awoke. As soon as I perceived this, I left my position and told the others that he would be all right. I started to walk down the mountain and away.

A few hundred yards down, the three watchers came hurtling after me. I did not run, but turned to face them.

"Yes?"

They hesitated. "He says you're not to leave."

"And you're going to stop me, are you?"

In the blink of an eye, my dagger was unsheathed.

"We're to stop you, yes."

"And how are you going to go about that?"

Nobody answered. They all knew that, even three to one, I could outfight them.

"We serve him," one eventually said. "He can only count on us. He says to stop you. At any cost. If we die in the process, so be it."

Immediately I dropped my dagger and held up my hands.

"Then seize me," I said. "Do it now, before I change my mind."

The three boys rushed in and twisted my arms behind my back, binding them there. They blindfolded me, gagged me, tied a rope around my neck, and led me in this humiliation back to his bedside, where they forced me to my knees. I felt my blindfold being lifted and looked into the eyes of the wounded man.

"I am disappointed," he said hoarsely. "You couldn't best these three?"

I said nothing. He laughed and put the cloth back over my eyes.

"Another illusion shattered," he said. "You are weak after all."

He motioned to the watchers, and I was led away, pushed and pulled and thrown into a cell, the door shut, the key turned.

For several paths of the moon I was left imprisoned. The watchers treated me tolerably; they shackled only one of my wrists to the wall; they fed me daily. But the nourishment was insufficient, the lack of sunlight debilitating, and my health suffered. His, on the other hand, improved. On the day of the memory that he fed me, unknown to me at the time, he crept into the prison one day and lurked in the shadows, deliberately listening to a hushed argument between the two watchers indoors:

"She's weakening. She might be dying. We've got to do something!"

"She left, didn't she? She deserves it."

"She sacrificed her freedom to spare our lives!"

"So she's weak."

"That's not weakness! We've got to tell him what she did!"

The next day he ordered my release. I did not call in to see him, as I painfully made my way back down the mountain, away from him.

Part 5

When we were rulers and we were happy, sometimes we would have evenings of games with friends. Our favourite was 'Magic'. Four players randomly chose one of four shields, each of which had a symbol on the front, denoting which character you were. The sheepskin meant you were the sheep; the crossed swords, the knight; the horn, the Viking; and the question mark, none of us knew. The aim was to battle for one another's sexual cells. In a sense it was foreplay, for he would become very demanding after a game of Magic. He loved the grandiosity of the game, the exhibition. He loved the exhibition especially. He liked to exhibition me. Once, in the theatre where the whole city was watching a play, he stopped the actors midway through, called for the attention of the audience, and had me perform fellatio on him, for them. When he had finished with me he calmly sat down and ordered the resumption of the play. He seemed engrossed but I couldn't follow it any more, not with the aftertaste of his semen in my mouth, and the throbbing of my clitoris. All the way through the agony of the play, I tried to figure out whether I was his lover or his slave.

And now, he is chasing me across a field. I know it was cursed long ago, but I have no choice but to cross it. As I step onto it, suddenly I become a mouse. My tiny legs pound the earth, but progress is slow. I see above me he has become a bird, catching up to me. We pass over the field, and at the other side, where we stand in the shadows of the beginning of the forest, we resume our human forms. He has caught up to me. I'm exhausted, and I turn to face him, and wait. Somehow I've realised that whatever he does now, I'm neither going to run nor hide any longer. He can do what he will – imprison me, fill my mind with memories and hallucinations until I lose it, publicly humiliate me, even kill me – but I will run no more. These thoughts must be pouring out of me; I can see from his expression and his stance that he comprehends.

"The terrible thing," he says quietly. I say nothing. My heart is racing, but I'm not afraid. "The terrible thing. I cursed this place myself. Cursed it to reveal terrible things to those who pass over it. And now I really have had one backfire on me, haven't I? Yes. I see it all now."

My breath quickens. I remain silent.

"You don't fear me any more."

He takes my silence as agreement.

"And if you don't fear me any more, then you-"

"-I don't."

He nods slowly. Is he crying? I feel ashamed just looking at him, thus broken.

"Take our children," he says.

"I will."

He turns away from me. "Good night, Josie."

A note from the book:

"Thanks to Mattias Forshage, Merl, and Paul Cowdell, for conceiving me.

Thanks to James Cameron, for taking me to task over the years.

Thanks to Eric Bragg, for making me exist.

And thanks to all the SLAGs in the world, because we all love slags. For more SLAG-work go to http://robberbridegroom.blogspot.com/."